真棒

Zhēn Bàng!

Workbook

Senior Advisor

王昭華 Margaret M. Wong

Director of International Education / Chinese Instructor
Breck School, Minneapolis, MN

Lead Author

方虹婷 Tiffany Fang

Master of Arts in Teaching Chinese as a Second Language

Contributing Writers

沈映佳 Shen Yingjia   陈淑华 Chen Shu-hwa   钱玲岑 Chien Ling-tsen

EMC Publishing

ST. PAUL • INDIANAPOLIS

Editorial Director
Alejandro Vargas

Associate Editor
Hannah da Veiga

Assistant Editor
Lei Han

Cover Designer
Leslie Anderson

Proofreader
International Contact, Inc

Care has been taken to verify the accuracy of information presented in this book. However, the authors, editors, and publisher cannot accept responsibility for Web, e-mail, newsgroup, or chat room subject matter or content, or for consequences from application of the information in this book, and make no warranty, expressed or implied, with respect to its content.

Credits: Photos and illustrations were provided by Live ABC Interactive Corporation.

We have made every effort to trace the ownership of all copyrighted material and to secure permission from copyright holders. In the event of any question arising as to the use of any material, we will be pleased to make the necessary corrections in future printings. Thanks are due to the aforementioned authors, publishers, and agents for permission to use the materials indicated.

ISBN 978-0-82195-768-4

875 Montreal Way
St. Paul, MN 55102
Email: educate@emcp.com
Website: www.emcschool.com

Printed in the United States of America

19 18 17 16 15 14 13 12 11 2 3 4 5 6 7 8 9 10

Table of Contents

Foundation A 1
Foundation B 8
Foundation C 16
Foundation D 23
Foundation E 30
Foundation F 36
Unit 1 Lesson A 43
Lesson B 50
Lesson C 57
Lesson D 65
Unit 2 Lesson A 71
Lesson B 80
Lesson C 86
Lesson D 93
Unit 3 Lesson A 99
Lesson B 105
Lesson C 112
Lesson D 118
Unit 4 Lesson A 125
Lesson B 132
Lesson C 139
Lesson D 146
Unit 5 Lesson A 153
Lesson B 160
Lesson C 167
Lesson D 175
Unit 6 Lesson A 182
Lesson B 190
Lesson C 197
Lesson D 204

名字：________________________ 日期：____________

Foundation A

1 Fill in the blanks with the correct answers according to the content of this lesson.

1. The biggest manmade structure in the world is ________________.
2. The capital of China is ________________.
3. ________________ and ________________ are the two main rivers in China.
4. ________________ and ________________ are regions with Chinese as the official language.
5. China is the most populated country in the world with around ________________ people.
6. ________________ is the biggest public square in the world.
7. Both China and the United States border the ________________ Ocean.

2 Complete the sentences in Pinyin for each situation below.

1. If you can't understand what your Chinese friend says, you may say to him / her…

____

2. If you are not sure about the tone of a word and want to ask your teacher, you can say…

____

3. If your classmate asks you the tone of a character and you are sure that it is the second tone, you may tell him / her…

____

4. Your friend asks you if today is Wednesday, but it is actually Tuesday. So, you reply…

____

5. Following the above question, if today is Wednesday, you say…

____

3 Look at the following three groups, and match the related texts to one another.

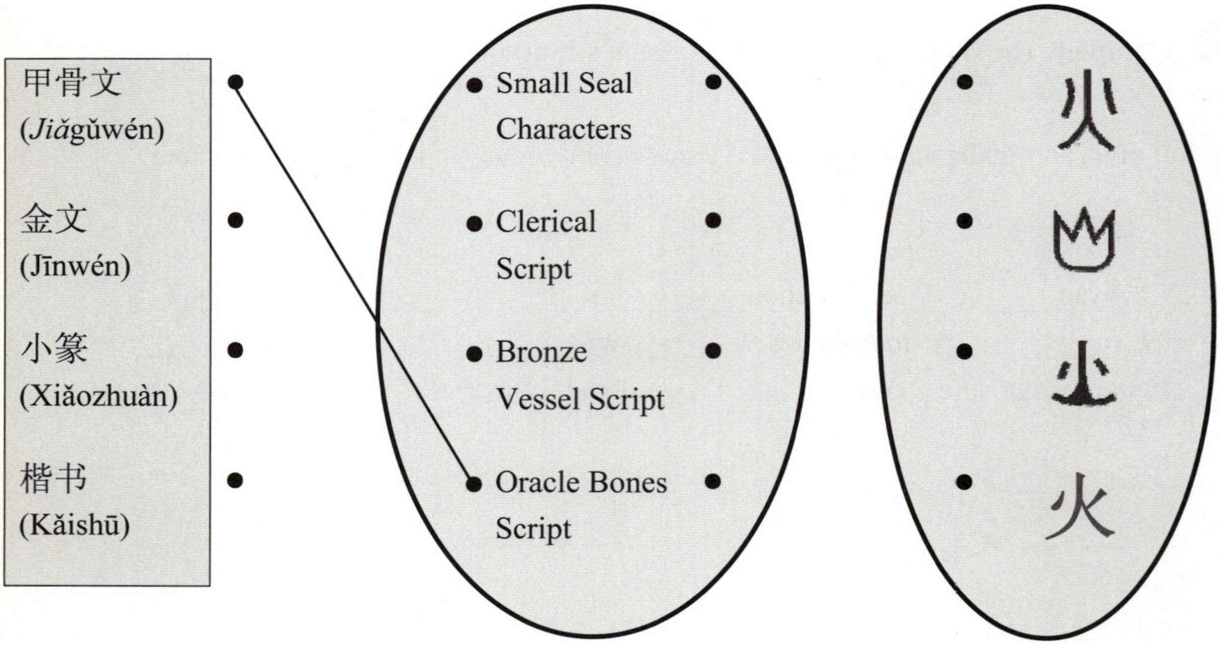

名字：________________________ 日期：____________

4 Find the radicals of the 20 Chinese words below using the clues (A-J) provided in the chart.

A. 山 shān 	C. 宀 mián 	E. 人 rén 	G. 貝 bèi 	I. 雨 yǔ 
B. 大 dà 	D. 口 kǒu 	F. 木 mù 	H. 土 tǔ 	J. 日 rì 

1. 他 tā
he ______

2. 天 tiān
sky ______

3. 岩 yán
rock ______

4. 坐 zuò
to sit ______

5. 森 sēn
forest ______

6. 早 zǎo
morning ______

7. 地 dì
land ______

8. 守 shǒu
to keep watch ______

9. 峽 xiá
gorge ______

10. 夫 fū
husband ______

11. 財 cái
wealth ______

12. 吃 chī
to eat ______

13. 樹 shù
tree ______

14. 雲 yún
cloud ______

15. 例 lì
example ______

16. 雪 xuě
snow ______

17. 明 míng
bright ______

18. 貨 huò
goods ______

19. 家 jiā
family ______

20. 吞 tūn
to swallow ______

名字：________________ 日期：________

5 Draw a line from the words in the center of the chart to the correct radical and meaning.

Radical	金 jīn	木 mù	艸 cǎo	水 shuǐ	目 mù
	1. 錢 qián	**2. 海 hǎi**	**3. 草 cǎo**	**4. 森 sēn**	**5. 眼 yǎn**
Meaning	sea	money	grass	eye	forest

6 Use the English definitions given and radicals A-J below to complete each character.

A. 言 (yán, *words*)
C. 犬 (犭) (quǎn, *dog*)
E. 水 (氵) (shuǐ, *water*)
G. 艸 (艹) (cǎo, *grass*)
I. 疒 (chuáng, *sick*)

B. 囗 (wéi, *around*)
D. 女 (nǚ, *woman*)
F. 火 (huǒ, *fire*)
H. 手 (扌) (shǒu, *hand*)
J. 辶 (chuò, *to go*)

1. *imprison*	3. *disease*	5. *younger sister*	7. *to speak*	9. *to escape*
_____ 人	_____ 丙	_____ 未	_____ 兑	_____ 兆
qiú	bǐng	mèi	shuō	táo

2. *to roast*	4. *dog*	6. *river*	8. *flower*	10. *to pull*
_____ 考	_____ 句	_____ 工	_____ 化	_____ 立
kǎo	gǒu	hé	huā	lā

名字：______________________________ 日期：______________

7 **The following is a Chinese myth. Read the story, and use its contents and the clues in parentheses to fill in the correct radical answers (A-W) in the blanks below.**

A. 木 mù	B. 石 shí	C. 水 shuǐ	D. 金 jīn	E. 大 dà	F. 門 mén
G. 手 shǒu	H. 虫 huǐ	I. 目 mù	J. 雨 yǔ	K. 貝 bèi	L. 女 nǚ
M. 刀 dāo	N. 口 kǒu	O. 日 rì	P. 火 huǒ	Q. 山 shān	R. 玉 yù
S. 土 tǔ	T. 米 mǐ	U. 人 rén	V. 田 tián	W. 犬 quǎn	

A Legend of Radicals

A long time ago, when there was not even one 邑(yì, *city*), there was a giant 1.______________ (*person; people*) in northern China whose 力(lì, *strength*) was as 2.______________ (*large; great*) as that of an 牛(niú, *ox*). At the time, there were many 3.______________ (*dog(s)*) and 4.______________ (*insect(s)*) that wanted to 食(shí, *to eat*) people with their 5.______________ (*knife*)-like 6.______________ (*mouth(s)*) so that the people had to hide in 广(yǎn, *shelter(s)*). In order to protect each 宀(mián, *roof; family*), the giant 辶(chuò, *to go; went*) on 足(zú, *foot*) to find the monsters. He then beat them with 7.______________ (*stone(s)*) in his 8.______________ (*hand(s)*). Later, the 9.______________ (*sun*), like 10.______________ (*fire*), dried up all the 11.______________ (*water*) and 草(cǎo, *grass*) on the 12.______________ (*earth; ground*), and all the 魚(yú, *fish*) in the rivers and the 禾(hé, *grain(s)*) in the 13.______________ (*field(s)*) died. Because there was no 14.______________ (*rice*) and 肉(ròu, *flesh; meat*) to eat and no

衣(yī, *clothes*) made of 糸(mì, *silk*) to wear, the people started to get 疒(chuáng, *sick*). After seeing this with his 15.______________ (*eye(s)*), the giant made a decision in his 心(xīn, *heart*) to grab the sun using his own hands and 囗(wéi, *close*) it behind a 16.____________________ (*door*) to listen to the 言(yán, *words*) of the people.

The giant was as fast as the 馬(mǎ, *horse(s)*) on land and the 鳥(niǎo, *bird(s)*) in the sky. Each 彳(chì, *pace*) he took was as wide as a 17.______________ (*mountain*). But the closer he got to the sun, the thirstier he became. Although he drank up several rivers, he still died. The giant's body became a large mountain, and the staff of 18.______________ (*wood*) he carried in his hands became a forest. The gods in the sky were moved by his spirit, so they let 19.______________ (*rain*) fall on the land below. The people returned to their lives, and the little boys and 20.______________ (*female(s)*) grew up.A long time later, a man with a 巾(jīn, *kerchief*) tied around his head appeared. He sat on a 車(chē, *cart*) and told this story to people while he 攴(pū, *tap(ped)*) out a rhythm with a 竹(zhú, *bamboo*) stick. The story was popular with 阜(fù, *plenty*) of people, and many paid him rare 21.______________ (*shell(s)*), 22.______________ (*jade*) or 23.______________ (*gold*) for him to perform, making him the richest person in the world.

名字：________________________ 日期：____________

8 **A telephone number is hidden in the girls' names in the list below. Find the girls names one by one, and write down the Pinyin and tone of each name. 1 stands for the first tone, 2 for the second, 3 for the third and 4 for the fourth. Use this to find the hidden telephone number, then write it down.**

Guest List	
1. Allen 亚伦	*5. Wendy* 温蒂
2. Penny 佩妮	*6. Jim* 吉姆
3. David 大卫	*7. Tom* 汤姆
4. Kelly 凯莉	*8. Lisa* 莉莎

Girl's name								
Pinyin and tone								
Telephone number								

9 **Write your Chinese name using both Pinyin and characters.**

我叫 (Wǒ jiào)____。

10 **Write the Chinese name of one of your classmates using both Pinyin and characters.**

他 / 她叫 (Tā / Tā jiào)____________________________________。

名字：________________ 日期：________

Foundation B

1 **The following activity is about the special names of some of China's provinces. Use the prompts given to fill in the names of the respective provinces.**

1. ______________

Its capital is China's largest car manufacturing city—leading it to also be known as the "city of cars."

Due to its tons of coal deposits, the province is known as a "sea of coal."

2. ______________

3. ______________

The province is known as the "oven" for its hot summers.

Its capital is famous for pottery, so it is also known as the "Porcelain Capital."

4. ______________

5. ______________

Because of its abundance of natural springs, this province is also called the "city of springs."

2 **Each Chinese province is unique. Below are the accounts of five people who are traveling in China. Read their comments to figure out where they are. Then, shade in the province they are in on the map below using the colors given. The last section is for you. Collect information on a province that has not been introduced, and write a few facts describing the province in the space provided. Then, color in the province on the map in a different color. Don't forget to draw a picture of yourself in the box!**

- It is China's southernmost province.
- There is a beautiful name for this place: Hawaii of the East.

Blue

Black

- The vast meadows make me feel free.
- The lake here is the largest inland saltwater lake in China.

Yellow

- It is both China's most northern and eastern province.
- The ice sculptures in the "city of ice" are really amazing!

- This province is the birthplace of Confucius.
- Tai Shan, the first natural and cultural World Heritage Site named in China, can be found here.

Green

Pink

- It has a historical name, the "province of abundance".
- Do you like giant pandas? If so, you must come visit them.

____

____

____

名字：________________ 日期：__________

3 Read the following situations and write what the teacher might say in Pinyin.

1. Class has begun. The teacher wishes for the students to open their textbooks, so he'll / she'll say…

   ____

2. When the teacher wishes for a student to stand, he'll / she'll say…

   ____

3. Following the above, to ask the student to sit back down, he'll / she'll say…

   ____

4. If the teacher wishes to teach something on the following page, he'll / she'll say…

   ____

5. The teacher has written something on the board. He wants the students to see what he has written, so he'll / she'll say…

   ____

6. Receiving a handout from the teacher, the students may want to say to the teacher…

   ____

4 Color the circles with Traditional Chinese characters red, and color circles with Simplified Chinese characters green.

轨 魷 項 鉛 饲 鳥 沦 樂 纪 間 谅 赏 動 貼 闷 覓 乐 诉 買

5 Match the Traditional Chinese character on the left with the same Simplified Chinese character on the right.

1. _____ 從	A. 后
2. _____ 禮	B. 难
3. _____ 適	C. 体
4. _____ 體	D. 从
5. _____ 後	E. 礼
6. _____ 塵	F. 尘
7. _____ 難	G. 适

名字：______________________ 日期：__________

6 **Each shaded box below has three characters that share the same radical; write it on the line provided.**

1. ______ 仕 付 从

5. ______ 仄 厅 历

2. ______ 宇 它 守

6. ______ 卫 叩 即

3. ______ 边 过 达

7. ______ 饥 饭 饮

4. ______ 古 可 兄

8. ______ 点 杰 烹

名字：________________ 日期：________

7 Each basic stroke has been given a symbol below. Use the symbols to represent the correct order and the correct strokes of each character. Follow the model.

横 héng (Horizontal stroke) → ●

竖 shù (Vertical stroke) → ▲

撇 piě (Left-slanted stroke) →■

捺 nà (Right-slanted stroke) → ★

点 diǎn (Dot) → ○

提 tí (Rising stroke) →△

钩 gōu (Hook) → □

折 zhé (Bent stroke) → ☆

Li.zi: 王：●●▲●

1. 入：________________

2. 七：________________

3. 日：________________

4. 手：________________

5. 江：________________

6. 信：________________

名字：________________________ 日期：____________

Foundation C

1 **Complete the following crossword puzzle with the Pinyin of the municipalities and special administration regions you learned about in this Foundation lesson.**

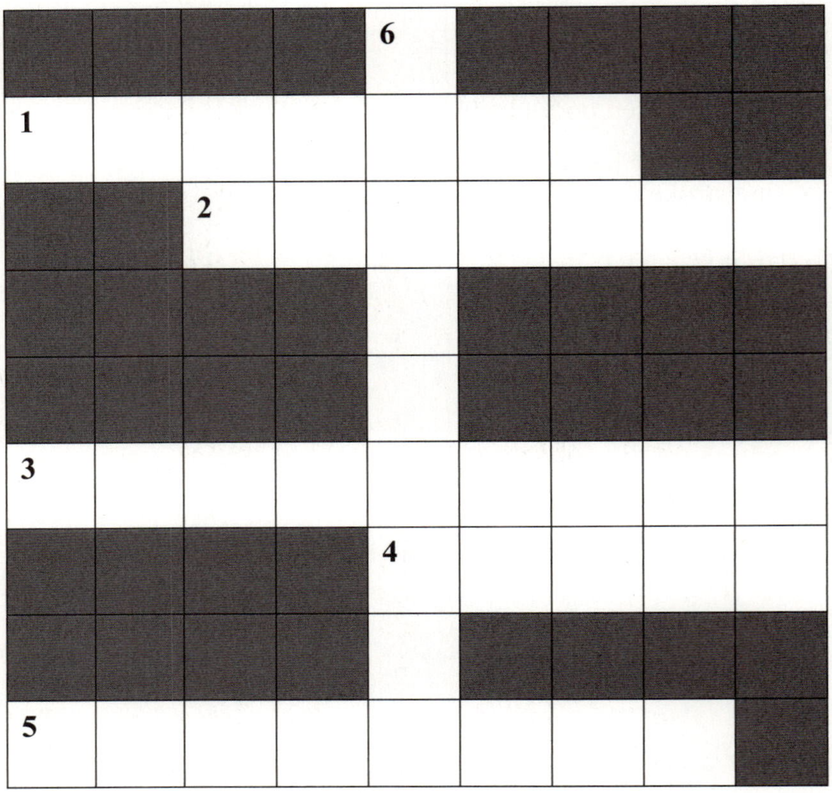

Across

1. It is the capital of the People's Republic of China (PRC).
2. It is called "the pearl of Bohai."
3. It is called the "city of mountains."
4. The Ruínas da Antiga Catedral de São Paulo can be found here.
5. It is a combination of the old and the new, the traditional and the contemporary.

Down

6. It is China's first Special Administrative Region.

2 **Use the hints given to figure out the names of the following cities. If the city is a municipality, color the circle next to the number red. If it is a Special Administration Region, color the circle blue.**

○ 1. ____________________

- A well-situated port city
- Set to host the World Expo in 2010

○ 2. ____________________

- English is one of the most used languages here
- One of Asia's four small dragons

○ 3. ____________________

- The Heavenly Fort
- The multi-national museum of architecture

○ 4. ____________________

- Portuguese is one of the languages spoken here
- Tourism is the main industry

○ 5. ____________________

- Known for its spicy hotpots
- A transportation hub for China's southeast

○ 6. ____________________

- Home of the famous Peking Man
- Host city of the 2008 Summer Olympics

名字：________________ 日期：________

3 Write your responses in Pinyin for each situation below.

1. If your friend asks you for your Chinese textbook and you happen to have it with you, you can say…

____

2. If your friend asks you for three red pens and you don't have them, you can say…

____

3. If your classmate asks for help on a math question and you want to make sure that he/she has understood, you can say…

____

4. If your classmate asks for help on a math question and you'd like to know if there are any other questions he/she needs help with, you can say…

____

5. You ask your classmate a question, but you don't understand what he/she said, you can say…

____

6. Your friend told you something and he/she wants to make sure if you understand. If you understand what they said, you can say…

____

4 Complete the dialogues according to the pictures.

Situation 1

A: 懂了吗？Dǒng .le .ma?

B: ______________________________。

Situation 2

A: 有问题吗？Yǒu wèntí .ma?

B: ______________________________。

Situation 3

A: 懂了吗？Dǒng .le .ma?

B: ______________________________。

Situation 4

A: 有问题吗？Yǒu wèntí .ma?

B: ______________________________。

名字：________________________ 日期：____________

5 **Look at the following three groups and match the related pictures, pictographs and characters to one another.**

鳥　人　魚　衣　羊　犬

6 **Write the first stroke of every character below in the boxes provided, then draw a line between the character in the first row and the character in the second row that share the same first stroke.**

井		尘		只		亡		会	

少		记		人		天		旦	

名字：________________ 日期：__________

7 **Look at the characters below and shade in the first stroke.**

1. 江	6. 司	11. 卡	16. 电
2. 土	7. 自	12. 尖	17. 合
3. 日	8. 豆	13. 文	18. 火
4. 刀	9. 王	14. 字	19. 行
5. 也	10. 上	15. 下	20. 父

名字：_______________ 日期：__________

Foundation D

1 **Label the map with the autonomous regions listed below, and then shade in each one with the color indicated.**

Inner Mongolia Autonomous Region: red
Xinjiang Uyghur Autonomous Region: blue
Guangxi Zhuang Autonomous Region: green
Tibet Autonomous Region: yellow
Ningxia Hui Autonomous Region: black

名字：______________________ 日期：__________

2 Imagine that you are a reporter who has just returned from visiting the five autonomous regions in China. Use your notes below to label and give an appropriate title for the location of each picture.

Notes
* Ningxia Hui Autonomous Region, cultivated by the Yellow River—rich in crops, pastures, and minerals
* Xingjiang Uyghur Autonomous Region, watched over by 1,000 Buddha—home of the melons
* Guangxi Zhuang Autonomous Region, the Zhuang tribe living on limestone topography
* Tibet Autonomous Region, the sunshine city in the Himalayas
* Inner Mongolia Autonomous Region, Mongolian culture on the grassland

1. Place name：______________________

Title：______________________

2. Place name：______________________

Title：______________________

3. Place name：______________________

Title：______________________

4. Place name: ______________________

Title: ______________________

5. Place name: ______________________

Title: ______________________

名字：______________________ 日期：__________

3 **Your class has a new Chinese exchange student named Ming. Help him understand what the teacher says by writing the English phrases below in Pinyin.**

1. The teacher says, "Please write your name on the board."

____

2. The teacher says, "Please repeat after me."

____

3. The teacher says, "Let's listen to the CD now."

____

4. The teacher says, "Please try it yourself."

____

5. The teacher says, "Please come here."

____

6. The teacher says, "Please say it again."

____

名字：______________________ 日期：__________

4 **Match the descriptions on the left to the ideographs in the center column by writing the appropriate letter in the space provided. Then draw a line between the ideographs and their meaning in the right-hand column.**

1. _______ In the likeliness of a person with his/her legs crossed

2. _______ In the likeliness of a person with his/her arms and legs wide open

3. _______ In the likeliness of a row of wheat

4. _______ In the likeliness of a person holding something under his/her armpits

5. _______ The short stroke represents the object's position in relation to the longer stroke

6. _______ In the likeliness of a flag placed in the middle of an area

A. 

B. 

C. 

D. 

E. 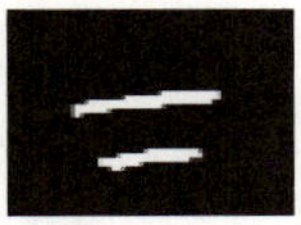

F. 

- 大 big
- 齊 neat
- 中 middle
- 夾 to clip
- 交 to interlock
- 下 downward

名字：________________________ 日期：__________

5 **Below are five 習 *xí* characters. Write down what font each might be on the lines provided.**

1. ________________

2. ________________

A. Seal style

B. Official style

C. Standard style

D. Running style

E. Cursive style

4. ________________

3. ________________

5. ________________

6 Write the letter of the sentence that corresponds to each illustration in the speech bubbles.

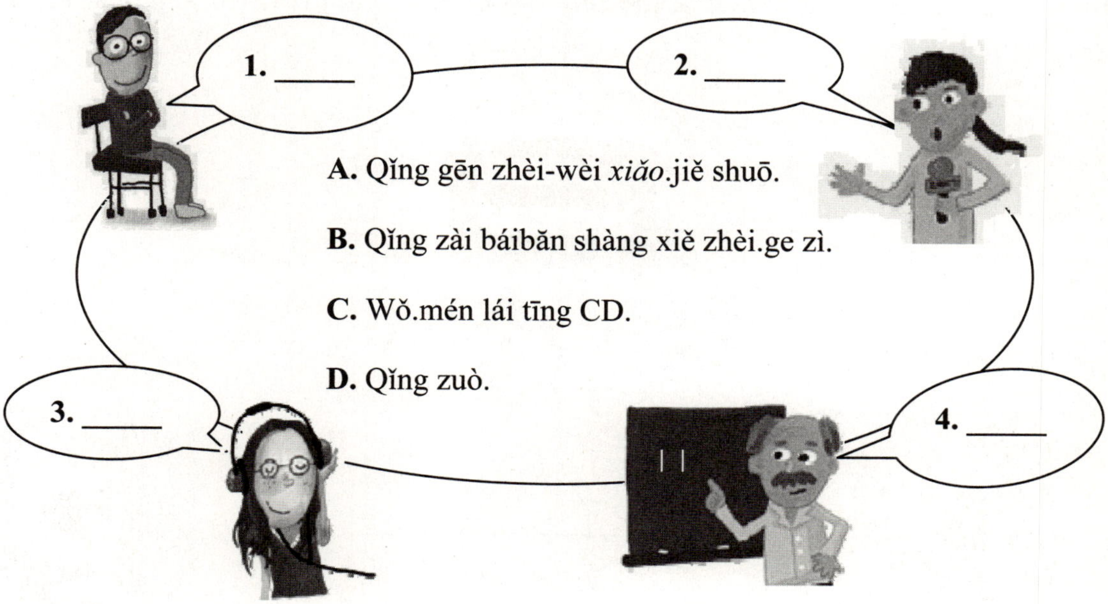

Foundation E

1 **The gray areas are Taiwan's cities. Color the municipalities red and the counties yellow. Write the English names of the counties on the lines provided and answer the four questions below.**

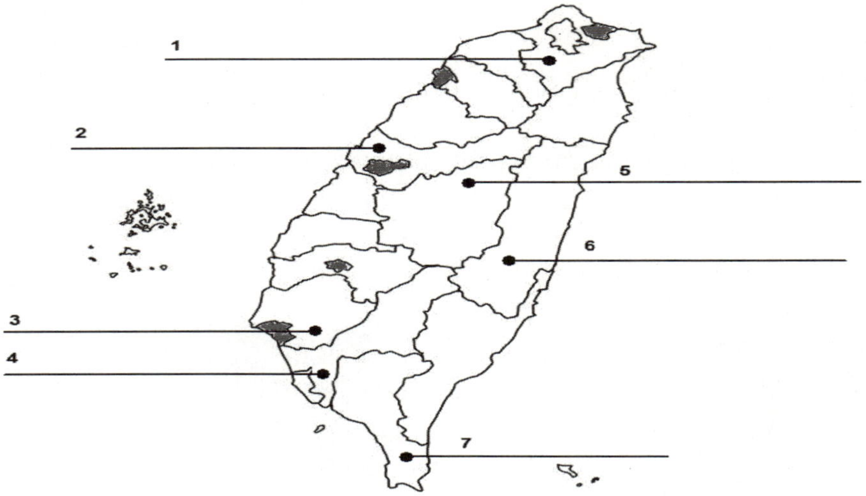

1. What are the other two languages spoken in Taiwan besides of Mandarin Chinese?

____

2. Which two seasons are the typhoon seasons in Taiwan?

____

3. What is the name of Taiwan's tallest mountain?

____

4. Taiwan is small, but its topography is varied. Why?

____

名字：________________ 日期：________

2 Fill in the place names according to the dialogues below.

1.

A: I am going to the highest mountain in Taiwan this summer.

B: Oh, do you mean ________________?

2.

A: What is the key industry in Taiwan?

B: ________________! The computers we are using now are from there!

3.

A: Do you know what Taiwan's capital city is?

B: Of course I know! It is ________________ City.

4.

A: My grandson brings me Oolong tea from Ali Mountain. It tastes so good!

B: Yes, tea is the No. 3 crop in Taiwan. The top two are __________________ and sugarcane, and they are also good.

5.

A: I don't quite understand characters used in Taiwan, why?

B: We use Simplified characters here in China, but people in Taiwan use __________________ characters.

6.

A: How many municipalities are there in Taiwan? What are they?

B: Two, one is __________________ City and the other one is __________________ City.

名字：______________________ 日期：__________

3 Answer the questions in Pinyin using the prompts given.

1. Nǐ shàng shén.me kè? (*Math*)

____

2. Zhè xuéqī nǐ xiū shén.me kè? (*Chinese and History*)

____

3. Hái yǒu wèntí .ma? (*No*)

____

4. "Huá" shì dì-jǐ shēng?

____

4 Match the combinations of each radical with the 马 *mǎ* phoneme with the appropriate English word.

1. _____ 虫 (*insect*) + 马 = 蚂 (mǎ)	A. *agate*
2. _____ 王 (*jade*) + 马 = 玛 (mǎ)	B. *ant*
3. _____ 石 (*stone*) + 马 = 码 (mǎ)	C. *yard (unit of measure)*
4. _____ 口 (*mouth*) + 口 + 马 = 骂 (mà)	D. *mother*
5. _____ 女 (*women*) + 马 = 妈 (mā)	E. *scold*

名字：______________________ 日期：__________

5 **Match the words below (combinations of pictograms or ideograms) to the definitions provided in the word bank.**

A. to be bright	F. fairy; saint
B. to be stuck	G. fire
C. to see	H. to be massive
D. to lie on one's face downward	I. to divide, to dissect
E. prisoner	J. man

1. _____ 日 (sun) + 月 (moon) = 明
2. _____ 田 (field) + 力 (strength) = 男
3. _____ 人 (people) + 山 (mountain) = 仙
4. _____ 人 (people) + 犬 (dog) = 伏
5. _____ 手 (hand) + 目 (eye) = 看
6. _____ 火 (fire) + 火 = 炎
7. _____ 口 (enclosure) + 人 (people) = 囚
8. _____ 石 (stone) + 石 + 石 = 磊
9. _____ 上 (up) + 下 (down) = 卡
10. _____ 木 (wood) + 斤 (ax) = 析

名字：________________________ 日期：____________

6 Select the structure type for each character.

A. top-bottom	C. left-right	E. stand alone
B. enclosed	D. semi-enclosed	

1. _____ 司
2. _____ 利
3. _____ 盆
4. _____ 子
5. _____ 图
6. _____ 历
7. _____ 北
8. _____ 思
9. _____ 超
10. _____ 女

7 Match each character on the left to the character with the same structure type on the right.

1. _____ 村	A. 进
2. _____ 山	B. 拆
3. _____ 回	C. 水
4. _____ 古	D. 国
5. _____ 例	E. 早
6. _____ 这	F. 湖

Foundation F

1 **The following are the statements of ten reporters on location. Use the keywords they provide to find the location of each reporter on the map on the next page and fill in the boxes with A-I.**

名字：______________________ 日期：__________

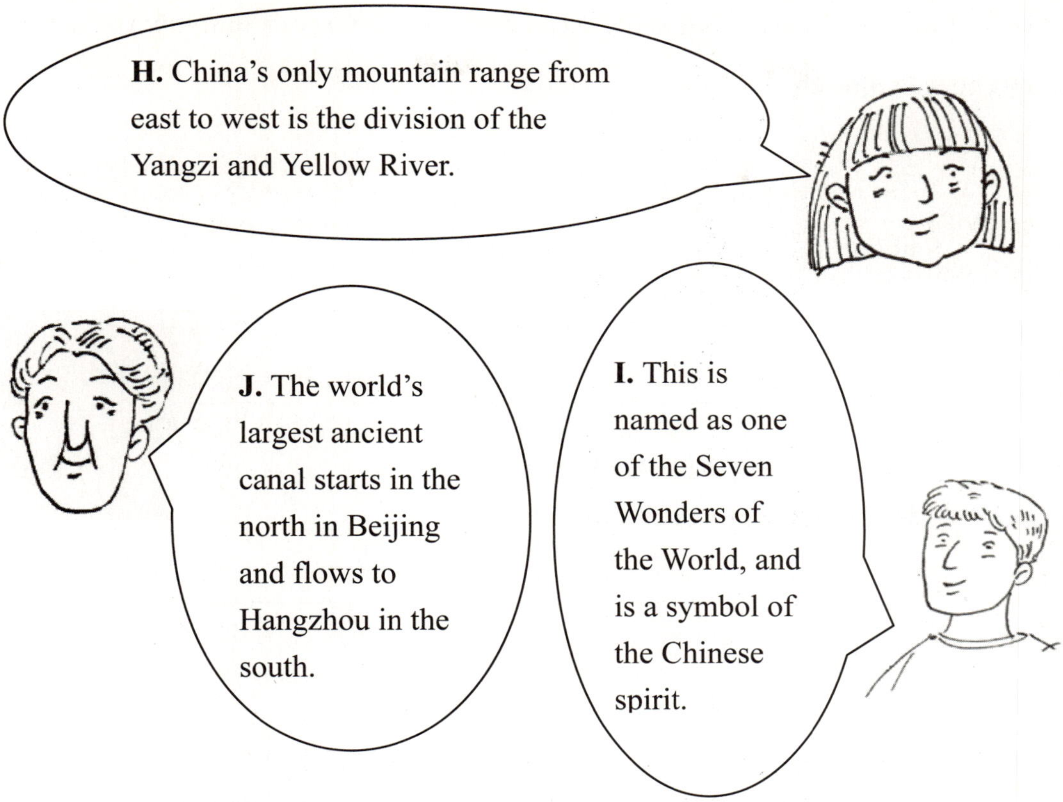

H. China's only mountain range from east to west is the division of the Yangzi and Yellow River.
J. The world's largest ancient canal starts in the north in Beijing and flows to Hangzhou in the south.
I. This is named as one of the Seven Wonders of the World, and is a symbol of the Chinese spirit.

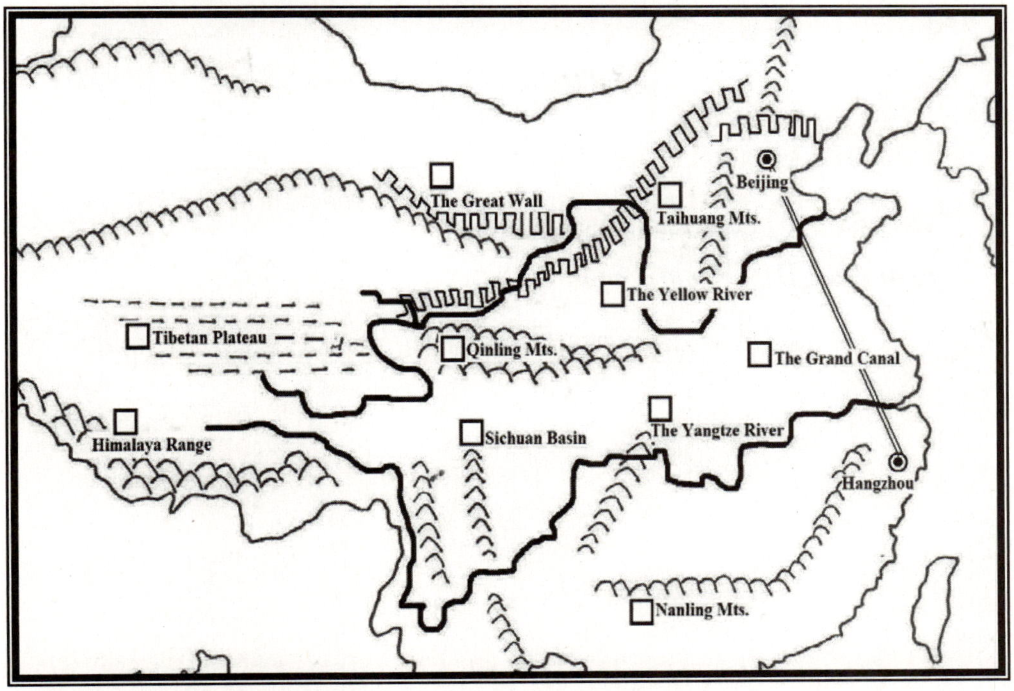

The Great Wall
Beijing
Taihuang Mts.
The Yellow River
Tibetan Plateau
Qinling Mts.
The Grand Canal
Himalaya Range
Sichuan Basin
The Yangtze River
Hangzhou
Nanling Mts.

2 Use the Pinyin of the words and sentences below as a reference to mark the actual tonal changes in speech.

1.

粉饼 (*compact foundation*)
fěnbǐng

____

买粉饼 (*to buy compact foundation*)
mǎi fěnbǐng

____

我买一个粉饼。Wǒ mǎi yí-.ge fěnbǐng.
(*I bought some compact foundation.*)

____

2.

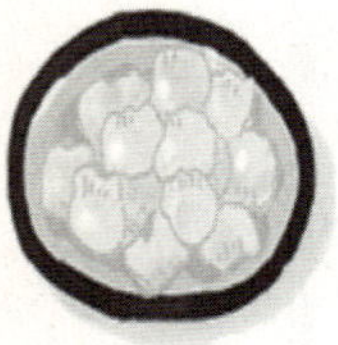

水饺 (*dumplings*)
shuǐjiǎo

____

煮水饺 (*to cook dumplings*)
zhǔ shuǐjiǎo

____

我想煮水饺。Wǒ xiǎng zhǔ shuǐjiǎo.
(*I'd like to cook some dumplings.*)

____

3. 小姐 (*miss*) xiǎo.jiě　　吕小姐 (*Miss Lu*) Lǚ xiǎo.jiě

________________　________________

吕小姐很窈窕。
Lǚ xiǎo.jiě hěn yǎotiǎo.
(*Miss Lu is very slim.*)

____

4. 演讲 (*to give a speech*) yǎnjiǎng　　演讲者 (*the speaker*) yǎnjiǎngzhě

________________　________________

我不喜欢第一个演讲者。
Wǒ bù xǐhuan dì-yī .ge yǎnjiǎngzhě.
(*I don't like being the first speaker.*)

____

5. 雨伞(*umbrella*) yǔsǎn　　小雨伞(*small umbrella*) xiǎo yǔsǎn

________________　________________

这不是一把小雨伞。Zhè bú shì yì-bǎ xiǎo yǔsǎn.
(*This is not a small umbrella.*)

____

名字：________________ 日期：________

3 Check to see if the following words and sentences follow the rules of Pinyin. If there are mistakes, circle them and write the correct Pinyin on top of the original.

1. dàxìang *(elephant)*

2. jǘzi *(orange)*

3. měiguó *(the U.S.A.)*

4. Zhōnggúo *(China)*

5. nühái *(girl)*

6. ōu xiānsheng *(Mr. Ou)*

7. xīngqīyī *(Monday)*

8. tā jiào hé kǎixī. *(Her name is Kaixi He.)*

9. wǒ shàng Zhōngweń kè. *(I take Chinese class.)*

10. Bàba, Māma wǎnān! *(Dad, mom, goodnight!)*

4 Use the Pinyin, radicals and English definitions of each set of words to differentiate whether or not they are derivative notation words. Write a (Y) for yes, and an (N) for no.

1. ( )

田 tián	男 nán
田	田
n. field	*n. man*

2. ( )

看 kàn	盲 máng
目	目
v. to see	*adj. blind*

3. ( )

追 zhuī	逐 zhú
辶	辶
v. to run after	*v. to pursue*

4. ( )

颠 diān	顶 dǐng
页	页
n. top	*adj. uppermost*

5. ( )

考 kǎo	老 lǎo
老	老
adj. old	*adj. aged*

6 ( )

白 bái	早 zǎo
白	日
n. white	*n. morning*

7. ( )

問 wèn	訊 xùn
口	言
v. to ask	*n. news*

8. ( )

疼 téng	痛 tòng
疒	疒
v. to cause pain	*v. to hurt*

5 Decide whether the words below are translations or transliterations. Answer letter A for translations, and B for transliterations.

1. _____ 电影 diànyǐng *movie*
2. _____ 派对 pàiduì *party*
3. _____ 太空人 tàikōngrén *astronaut*
4. _____ 汽车 qìchē *car*
5. _____ 马拉松 mǎlāsōng *marathon*
6. _____ 芭蕾 bālěi *ballet*
7. _____ 计算器 jìsuànqì *calculator*
8. _____ 比基尼 bǐjīní *bikini*
9. _____ 坦克 tǎnkè *tank*
10. _____ 飞机 fēijī *airplane*
11. _____ 模特 mó.tè *model*
12. _____ 空调 kōngtiáo *air conditioner*

名字：________________________ 日期：__________

6 **Use the hints from the English sentences to write the missingsentences on the blanks in Pinyin and recover what the Chinese teacher Miss Smith said in class.**

Miss Smith:

Good morning, everyone! 1.______________, on the board are vocabulary that we went over yesterday, 2.______________, practice writing each word five times on a piece of paper. Leo, 3.______________, your bag is taking up the whole desk. How do you plan on writing like that? Finally, let's talk about homework. 4.______________. The first exercise is very simple. 5.______________ turn to page 36; the answer is right there on the page. 6.______________ find out where the Great Wall and the Grand Canal is. After you find them, 7.______________, write on a separate piece of paper. Amy Wang, 8.______________. Don't talk on the phone in class!

(*The bell rings*)

Oh! Class is over! 9.______________! Homework for next time is on the white board. Please remember to do it.

名字：________________ 日期：__________

Unit 1 Lesson A

1 Write the following words in Pinyin.

 ____________

1. teacher

 ____________

2. principal

 ____________

3. Mrs.

 ____________

4. Mr.

 ____________

5. Miss

 ____________

6. I

 ____________

7. you

 ____________

8. you (plural)

2 Write the meaning of each word and then the correct Pinyin.

1. 早安 __________ __________
2. 名字 __________ __________
3. 叫 __________ __________
4. 什么 __________ __________
5. 你好 __________ __________
6. 你们 __________ __________
7. 姓 __________ __________
8. 我 __________ __________

3 Fill in the blanks with the appropriate Pinyin word from the box.

1. 你叫 Nǐ jiào________________名字 míng.zì?
2. 您贵 Nín guì________________?
3. 张 Zhāng________________，早安 zǎo’ān。
4. 我叫白苹 Wǒ jiào Bái Píng，________________?
5. ________________廖先生 Liào xiān.shēng。
6. 我的 Wǒ.de________________是林华 shì Lín Huá。

名字 míng.zì
什么 shén.me
这是 zhè shì
你呢 nǐ .ne
先生 xiān.shēng
姓 xìng

4 Unscramble the words and phrases below to make complete sentences.

Li.zi: 是 shì / 张国华 Zhāng Guóhuá / 这 zhè。
这是张国华。 Zhè shì Zhāng Guóhuá.

1. 什么 shén.me / 你 nǐ / 姓 xìng?

____

2. 名字 míng.zì / 你 nǐ / 什么 shén.me / 叫 jiào?

____

3. 林校长 Lín xiàozhǎng / 是 shì / 这 zhè。

____

4. 叫 jiào / 我 wǒ / 白苹 Bái Píng。

____

5 Choose the Chinese expression from the box that best fits each situation.

A. 早安。 Zǎo'ān.
B. 我姓白，你呢？ Wǒ xìng Bái, nǐ .ne?
C. 我姓张，叫国华。 Wǒ xìng Zhāng, jiào Guóhuá.

1.

2.

3.

6 Match each sentence on the left with the correct response on the right.

1. _____ 林老师，早安！
   Lín lǎoshī, zǎo'ān!
2. _____ 她(*she*)叫什么名字？
   Tā jiào shén.me míng.zì?
3. _____ 你好！我叫白苹，你呢？
   Nǐ hǎo! Wǒ jiào Bái Píng, nǐ .ne?
4. _____ 您贵姓？
   Nín guì xìng?
5. _____ 吴先生，你好。
   Wú xiān.shēng, *nǐ* hǎo.

A. 我叫张国华。
   Wǒ jiào Zhāng Guóhuá.

B. 我姓吴。
   Wǒ xìng Wú.

C. 你好。
   Nǐ hǎo.

D. 你们早。
   Nǐ.mén zǎo.

E. 她(*she*)叫林芳。
   Tā jiào Lín Fāng.

7 Answer the following in Pinyin.

1. 早安！ Zǎo'ān!

____

2. 你好。 *Nǐ* hǎo.

____

3. 你叫什么名字？ Nǐ jiào shén.me míng.zì?

____

8 **Imagine you are meeting 张华 Zhāng Huá, an exchange student from China, for the first time. Complete your conversation in Pinyin and make sure the dialogue follows a logical sequence.**

你 nǐ：______________________________

张华 Zhāng Huá：早安！ Zǎo'ān!

你 nǐ：______________________________

张华 Zhāng Huá：我姓张，叫张华。你呢？ Wǒ xìng Zhāng, jiào Zhāng Huá. Nǐ .ne?

你 nǐ：______________________________

(*Your good friend - Bai Ping - approaches you.*)

白苹 Bái Píng：早安。 Zǎo'ān.

张华 Zhāng Huá：早。 Zǎo.

你 nǐ：______________________________

白苹 Bái Pín：你好。你叫什么名字？ *Nǐ* hǎo. Nǐ jiào shén.me míng.zi̱?

张华 Zhāng Huá：我叫张华。 Wǒ jiào Zhāng Huá.

9 Complete each statement based on the picture and the clues.

1. This is 芳书 Fāngshū's father, so 芳书 Fāngshū's full name is:

   ____

林国安
Lín
Guó'ān

张华校长
Zhāng Huá
Xiàozhǎng

2. In this situation, they may greet each other:

   张华：______________________________

   林国安：______________________________

3. The girl's surname is:

   ____

   And her first name is:

   ____

10 Decide if the following statements are true or false. Correct any false statements.

1.______ Like Western society, children usually take their father's last name.

____

2.______ Chinese people are very friendly, so they usually introduce themselves by giving their first names.

____

3.______ Chinese names are divided into three parts: first name, middle name and last name.

____

4.______ When Chinese people give out business cards, they deliver them with both hands to show respect.

____

11 Write a greeting card to introduce yourself to the classmate sitting next to you. The card should include your Chinese name and the way to contact you. Don't forget to ask his/her name. Give it some design to make it stylish!

名字：______________________ 日期：__________

Unit 1 Lesson B

1 How do you greet your friends at the following times?

1.

____

2.

____

3.

____

4.

____

2 Write the meaning of each word and then the correct Pinyin.

1. 不好 __________ __________
2. 不错 __________ __________
3. 不去 __________ __________
4. 不见 __________ __________
5. 不行 __________ __________
6. 不睡觉 __________ __________
7. 不太贵 __________ __________
8. 不很好 __________ __________

3 Change the following sentences into questions by using 吗 *ma*.

Li.zi: 我是王老师。 Wǒ shì Wáng lǎoshī.

你是王老师吗？ Nǐ shì Wáng lǎoshī .ma?

1. 我们上课。 Wǒ.mén shàng-kè.

____

2. 她是林小姐。 Tā shì Lín xiǎo.jiě.

____

3. 张老师很好。 Zhāng lǎoshī hěn hǎo.

____

4. 校长姓张。 Xiàozhǎng xìng Zhāng.

____

4 Where do you need to be at the following times? Answer using the pattern 得…了 *děi .le* and the clues provided.

1. 11:00 P.M. (at home) ________________________
2. 4:00 A.M. (at the school gate) ________________________

名字：________________ 日期：________

5 Unscramble the words or phrases to make complete sentences.

Lì.zi: 他 tā / 好 hǎo / 不 bù / 太 tài
他不太好。 Tā bú tài hǎo.

1. 吗.ma / 上课 shàng-kè / 你 nǐ

____

2. 累 lèi / 你们 nǐ.mén / 很 hěn

____

3. 得 děi / 睡觉 shuì-jiào / 了.le / 你 nǐ

____

6 Fill in the blanks with the appropriate words from the box.

1. 你很累 Nǐ hěn lèi ____________?
2. ____________不见 bú jiàn。
3. 我不太好 Wǒ bú tài hǎo，我 wǒ ____________。
4. 王校长 Wáng xiàozhǎng ____________不好 bù hǎo。
5. 你 Nǐ ____________睡觉了 shuì-jiào .le。

很 hěn
好久 *hǎo* jiǔ
生病了 shēngbìng .le
吗.ma
得 děi

7 Match each question or statement with the correct response from the right.

1. _____ 你累吗？ Nǐ lèi .ma?
2. _____ 晚上好。 Wăn.shàng hăo.
3. _____ 下午好吗？ Xià.wŭ hăo .ma?
4. _____ 我得睡觉了。 *Wŏ* dĕi shuì-jiào .le.
5. _____ 我得走了。 *Wŏ dĕi* zŏu .le.

A. 晚安。 Wăn'ān.
B. 还行。 Hái xíng.
C. 不累。 Bú lèi.
D. 再见。 Zàijiàn.
E. 晚上好。 Wăn.shàng hăo.

8 Choose the correct sentence from the right column to finish the dialogue on the left.

1. A: 你好，好久不见。 Nǐ hăo, hăo jiŭ bú jiàn.

   B: ______________________________。

2. A: 我很好，你呢？ Wŏ hĕn hăo, nǐ .ne?

   B: ______________________________。

3. A: ______________________________吗 .ma?

   B: 我不太好。 Wŏ bú tài hăo.

4. A: 你很累，你不回家吗？ Nǐ hĕn lèi, nǐ bù huí-jiā .ma?

   B: 不回家 Bù huí-jiā，______________________________。

最近还行 Zuì jìn hái xíng
你生病了 Nǐ shēngbìng .le
我得上课了 *Wŏ* dĕi shàng-kè .le
好久不见 *Hăo* jiŭ bú jiàn

9 Choose the best response for each dialogue.

1. ______

A: 好久不见。 *Hǎo* jiǔ bú jiàn.

B: a. 我很累。 *Wǒ* hěn lèi.

b. 你得走了。 Nǐ *děi* zǒu .le.

c. 好久不见。 *Hǎo* jiǔ bú jiàn.

2. ______

A: 我得走了。 *Wǒ děi* zǒu .le.

B: a. 你好。 *Nǐ* hǎo.

b. 谢谢。 Xiè.x.

c. 一会儿见。 Yíhuìr jiàn.

3. ______

A: 最近好吗？ Zuìjìn hǎo .ma?

B: a. 不太好。 Bú tài hǎo.

b. 我得走了。 *Wǒ děi* zǒu .le.

c. 早上好。 Zǎo.shàng hǎo.

4. ______

A: 李校长累吗？Lǐ xiàozhǎng lèi .ma?

B: a. 不好。 Bù hǎo.

b. 不太累。 Bú tài lèi.

c. 很好。 *Hěn* hǎo.

10 Below are two text messages between Chen Hua and Zhang Fang. Read them and answer the following questions.

陈华，我下午不去，我得回家。明天去，好吗？
Chén Huá, wǒ xià.wǔ bú qù, wǒ děi huí-jiā. Míng.tiān qù, hǎo .ma?

张芳 Zhāng Fāng

张芳，早上好。好，明天去，明天见。
Zhāng Fāng, zǎo.shàng hǎo. Hǎo, míng.tiān qù, míng.tiān jiàn.

陈华 Chén Huá

1. 张芳下午去吗？ Zhāng Fāng xià.wǔ qù .ma?

____

2. 张芳下午上课吗？ Zhāng Fāng xià.wǔ shàng-kè .ma?

____

3. 陈华明天去不去？ Chén Huá míng.tiān qù .bú .qù?

____

11 Answer the following questions according to the picture on the left.

1. 他是林老师吗？ Tā shì Lín lǎoshī .ma?

____

2. 他好吗？ Tā hǎo .ma?

____

12 Decide if the statements are true or false. Correct any false statements.

1. In ancient China, people followed complex rules in greeting each other.

____

2. Smiling at another person or hugging was the way people in ancient China greeted each other.

____

3. The greeting 吃了没 *chī .le méi* developed because Chinese people pay a lot of attention to good food.

____

4. For the younger generation, they seldom use the greeting 吃了没 *chī .le méi* and say 你好 *Nǐ hǎo* instead.

____

13 Write a text message in Pinyin to tell your classmate that you are not going to class because you are sick.

名字：______________________ 日期：__________

Unit 1 Lesson C

1 **Fill in the blanks with the name of the country and the nationality.**

2 Fill in the blanks with the words from the box.

人 rén	朋友 péng.yǒu	不是 bú.shì
我的 wǒ.de	也 yě	大家 dàjiā

1. ____________________ 好 hǎo，我是加拿大人 wǒ shì Jiā'nádàrén。
2. 他们是英国人 Tā.mén shì Yīng.guórén，____________________ 美国人 Měi.guórén。
3. 我认识印度 Wǒ rèn.shì Yìndù ____________________。
4. 王校长是西班牙 Wáng xiàozhǎng shì Xībānyá ____________________。
5. Paul ____________________ 是新加坡人 shì Xīnjiāpōrén。
6. ____________________ 朋友很高兴 péng.yǒu hěn gāoxìng。

3 Change the following sentences to the plural form.

Lì.zi:
我是中国人。 Wǒ shì Zhōng.guórén.
我们是中国人。 Wǒ.mén shì Zhōng.guórén.

1. 他不是德国人。 Tā bú.shì Dé.guórén.

____

2. 她很高兴。 Tā hěn gāoxìng.

____

3. 你也是日本人。 *Nǐ* yě shì Rìběnrén.

____

4. 很高兴认识你。 Hěn gāoxìng rèn.shì nǐ.

____

4 Unscramble the words and phrases below to make complete sentences.

Lì.zi: 很 hěn / 老师 lǎoshī / 好 hǎo。

老师很好。 Lǎoshī *hěn* hǎo.

1. 也 yě / 我 wǒ / 加拿大 Jiā'nádà / 是 shì / 人 rén。

____

2. 我 wǒ / 日本人 Rìběnrén / 是 shì。

____

3. 哪国人 něi-guó rén / 是 shì / 你 nǐ / 请问 qǐngwèn？

____

4. 朋友 péng.yǒu / 我的 wǒ.de / 意大利 Yìdàlì / 是 shì / 人 rén。

____

5 Choose the correct phrase from the right to complete the dialogues on the left.

1. **A:** 我是美国人。 Wǒ shì Měi.guórén.

   B: 我 Wǒ ______________________。

2. **A:** 你是 Nǐ shì ______________________?

   B: 我是意大利人。Wǒ shì Yìdàlìrén.

3. **A:** 我是韩国人。 Wǒ shì Hán.guórén.

   B: 我 Wǒ ______________________。

4. **A:** 我的名字叫董军。 Wǒ.de míng.zì jiào Dǒng Jūn.

   B: ______________________。

不是美国人 bú.shì Měi.guórén
也是韩国人 yě shì Hán.guórén
很高兴认识你 hěn gāoxìng rèn.shì nǐ
哪国人 něi-guó rén

6 Answer the following questions.

1. 你的老师是哪国人？ Nǐ.de lǎoshī shì něi-guó rén?

   ____

2. Michael Jackson 是英国人吗？ Michael Jackson shì Yīng.guórén .ma?

   ____

3. 我是法国人，你呢？ Wǒ shì Fǎ.guórén, nǐ .ne?

   ____

7 Match each sentence on the left with the correct response on the right.

1. _____ 你是哪国人？

   Nǐ shì něi-guó rén?

2. _____ 他们的朋友姓什么？

   Tā.mén.de péng.yǒu xìng shén.me?

3. _____ 他是西班牙人吗？

   Tā shì Xībānyárén .ma?

4. _____ 很高兴认识你。

   Hěn gāoxìng rèn.shì nǐ.

5. _____ 我叫林书芳。

   Wǒ jiào Lín Shūfāng.

A. 你是中国人吗?

   Nǐ shì Zhōng.guórén .ma?

B. 我是法国人。

   Wǒ shì Fǎ.guórén.

C. 不是，他是意大利人。

   Bú.shì, tā shì Yìdàlìrén.

D. 她姓张。

   Tā xìng Zhāng.

E. 我也很高兴认识你。

   Wǒ yě hěn gāoxìng rèn.shì nǐ.

8 Complete the following sentences using 也 *yě* and the provided information.

1. Paul 是西班牙人。 Paul shì Xībānyárén. (Freda)

   ____

2. Larry 姓 Brown。 Larry xìng Brown. (Kevin)

   ____

3. 她叫白华。 Tā jiào Bái Huá. (他 tā)

   ____

4. 我认识新加坡人。 Wǒ rèn.shì Xīnjiāpōrén. (张先生 Zhāng xiān.shēng)

____

5. 小林是日本人。 Xiǎolín shì Rìběnrén. (大国 Dàguó)

____

6. 王校长是美国人。 Wáng xiàozhǎng shì Měi.guórén. (董老师 Dǒng lǎoshī)

____

9 Change the following sentences into questions. Make sure that the underlined part of the sentence given is the answer to the question. Follow the model.

Lì.zi: 我是<u>中文</u>老师。 Wǒ shì Zhōngwén lǎoshī.
你是<u>什么</u>老师？ Nǐ shì shén.me lǎoshī?

1. 他是<u>法</u>国人。 Tā shì <u>Fǎ</u>.guórén.

____

2. 我姓<u>高</u>。 Wǒ xìng <u>Gāo</u>.

____

3. 她的名字叫<u>林书芳</u>。 Tā.de míng.zì jiào <u>Lín Shūfāng</u>.

____

4. 他们认识新加坡朋友。 Tā.mén rèn.shì Xīnjiāpō péng.yǒu.

____

5. 林先生也认识张老师。 Lín xiān.shēng yě rèn.shì Zhāng lǎoshī.

____

10 Correct the following sentences. Follow the model.

Li.zi: 我是美国。 Wǒ shì Měi.guó.
我是美国人。 Wǒ shì Měi.guórén.

1. 我是德国人，你是德国人也吗？ Wǒ shì Dé.guórén, nǐ shì Dé.guórén yě .ma?

____

2. 我们是马来西亚人，你吗？ Wǒ.mén shì Mǎláixīyàrén, nǐ .ma?

____

3. 他们是什么国人？ Tā.mén shì shén.me guó rén?

____

4. 他认识法国人朋友。 Tā rèn.shì Fǎ.guórén péng.yǒu.

____

11 Decide if the following statements are true or false. Correct any false ones.

1. _____ Chinese titles may affect a person's age, social standing, and gender.

   ____

2. _____ The literal meaning of China is "big country."

   ____

3. _____ During the Tang Dynasty, China influenced the Mideast's economic and social systems.

   ____

12 You want to friend a Chinese person on Facebook, so you write a brief introduction in Pinyin about yourself as you send the request. Make sure you greet them and then write your name and nationality.

13 The person to whom you wrote accepted your request and wrote you back. Write how this person might respond to you. For example, he or she greets you, states his or her nationality and says "Nice to meet you."

名字：______________________ 日期：__________

Unit 1 Lesson D

1 Fill in the blanks with the numbers in Chinese characters to complete the sequences.

1. 零，________，二，三，________，五，________，七。
2. 十一，________，十五，________，________。
3. 二，________，六，________，________。
4. 十，________，________，________，五十。
5. 三十，________，九十。
6. 一，________，五，________，________。

2 Fill in the blanks on the left with the words from the box on the right.

1. 你们上 Nǐ.mén shàng ____________年级 niánjí？
2. 他 Tā ____________ 物理课 wùlǐ kè。
3. 十二岁上六 Shí'èr-suì shàng liù ____________。
4. 中文是 Zhōngwén shì ____________。
5. 我十七岁 Wǒ shíqī-suì，我是 wǒ shì ____________。
6. 他是一个 Tā shì yí-.ge ____________ 老师 lǎoshī。
7. 合唱团在(zài; *in*)音乐 Héchàngtuán zaì yīnyuè ____________。
8. 中国的初中一年级是美国的 Zhōng.guó .de chūzhōng yī-niánjí shì Měi.guó.de____________。

上 shàng
几 jǐ
数学 shùxué
年级 niánjí
教室 jiàoshì
外语 wàiyǔ
七年级 qī-niánjí
高中生 gāozhōngshēng

名字：______________________________ 日期：______________

3 Classify the following subjects in the categories indicated in the diagram.

中文 Zhōngwén	历史 lìshǐ	生物 shēngwù	法语 *Fǎ*yǔ	体育 tǐyù
美术 měishù	音乐 yīnyuè	地理 dìlǐ	文学 wénxué	物理 wùlǐ
信息技术 xìnxī jìshù	数学 shùxué	通用技术 tōngyòng jìshù	西班牙语 Xībānyáyǔ	计算机科学 jìsuànjī kēxué

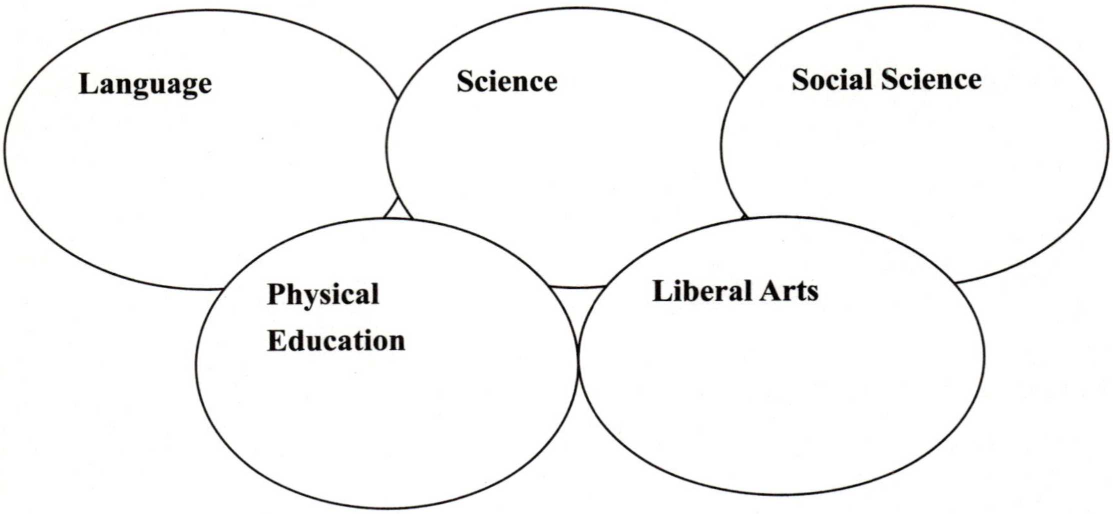

4 Match each sentence on the left with the correct response on the right.

1. _____ 这是法语教室吗？ Zhè shì Fǎyǔ jiàoshì .ma?
2. _____ 请问您多大？ Qǐngwèn nín duō dà?
3. _____ 他上化学课吗？ Tā shàng huàxué kèn .ma?
4. _____ 他们上几年级？ Tā.mén shàng jǐ-niánjí?
5. _____ 你学外语吗？ Nǐ xué wàiyǔ .ma?

A. 八十岁。 Bā.shí-suì.

B. 对，他上化学课。 Duì, tā shàng huàxué kè.

C. 对，我学西班牙语。 Duì, wǒ xué Xībānyáyǔ.

D. 十年级。 Shí-niánjí.

E. 不，这是地理教室。 Bù, zhè shì dìlǐ jiàoshì.

名字：______________________ 日期：__________

5 Unscramble the words or phrases to make complete sentences.

Lì.zi: 很 hěn / 老师 lǎoshī / 好 hǎo。
老师很好。 Lǎoshī *hěn* hǎo.

1. 几 jǐ / 他 tā / 上 shàng / 年级 niánjí?

____

2. 德语 Déyǔ / 他们 tā.mén / 上 shàng / 也 yě。

____

3. 哪国 něi-guó / 你 nǐ / 请问 qǐngwèn / 是 shì / 人 rén?

____

4. 朋友 péng.yǒu / 我的 wǒ.de / 得 děi / 中文 Zhōngwén / 上 shàng / 了 .le。

____

5. 历史 lìshǐ / 他们 tā. mén / 课 kè / 上 shàng。

____

6. 中文 Zhōngwén / 是 shì / 林 Lín / 老师 lǎoshī / 你的 nǐ.de / 老师 lǎoshī。

____

6 Change the following sentences into questions making sure that the underlined part is the answer to the question. Follow the model.

Li.zi: 欧阳明上<u>九</u>年级。 Ōuyáng Míng shàng <u>jiǔ</u>-niánjí.
欧阳明上几年级。 Ōuyáng Míng shàng jǐ-niánjí?

1. 这是<u>中文</u>教室。 Zhè shì <u>Zhōngwén</u> jiàoshì.

   ____

2. 我<u>十七</u>岁。 Wǒ <u>shíqī</u>-suì.

   ____

3. 小林上<u>法语</u>课。 Xiǎo Lín shàng <u>*Fǎ*yǔ</u> kè.

   ____

4. <u>对</u>，我是日本人。 <u>Duì</u>, wǒ shì Rìběnrén.

   ____

7 What class are you in at the following times? Write the name of the class in the space provided.

1. Monday, 9:00 A.M. ________________
2. Wednesday, 9:40 A.M. ________________
3. Friday, 10:30 A.M. ________________

4. Tuesday, 11:00 A.M. ________________

5. Monday, 1:50 P.M. ________________

6. Thursday, 2:00 P.M. ________________

7. Friday, 2:45 P.M. ________________

8 Answer the following questions based on the picture.

1. 他们几岁？ Tā.mén jǐ-suì?

____

2. 他们上高中二年级，对不对？
Tā.mén shàng gāozhōng èr-niánjí, duì .bú .duì?

____

9 Decide if the following statements are true or false. Correct any false ones.

1. _____ The compulsory education in China has been nine years since 1986.

____

2. _____ The most popular foreign language in high schools in China is Japanese.

____

3. _____ Children ages two to six can receive free preschool education in kindergarten.

____

10 Answer the following questions in Pinyin.

1. 你上几年级？ Nǐ shàng jǐ-niánjí?

____

2. 你几岁？ *Nǐ* jǐ-suì?

____

3. 你上什么外语课？ Nǐ shàng shén.me wàiyǔ kè?

____

4. 你的学校有什么外语课？ Nǐ.de xuéxiào yǒu shén.me wàiyǔ kè?

____

5. 你上西班牙语吗？ Nǐ shàng Xībānyáyǔ .ma?

____

6. 你的老师不是美国人，对不对？ Nǐ.de lǎoshī .bú shì Měi.guórén, duì .bú .duì?

____

名字：________________ 日期：________

Unit 2 Lesson A

1 Complete the diagram below and answer the questions that follow.

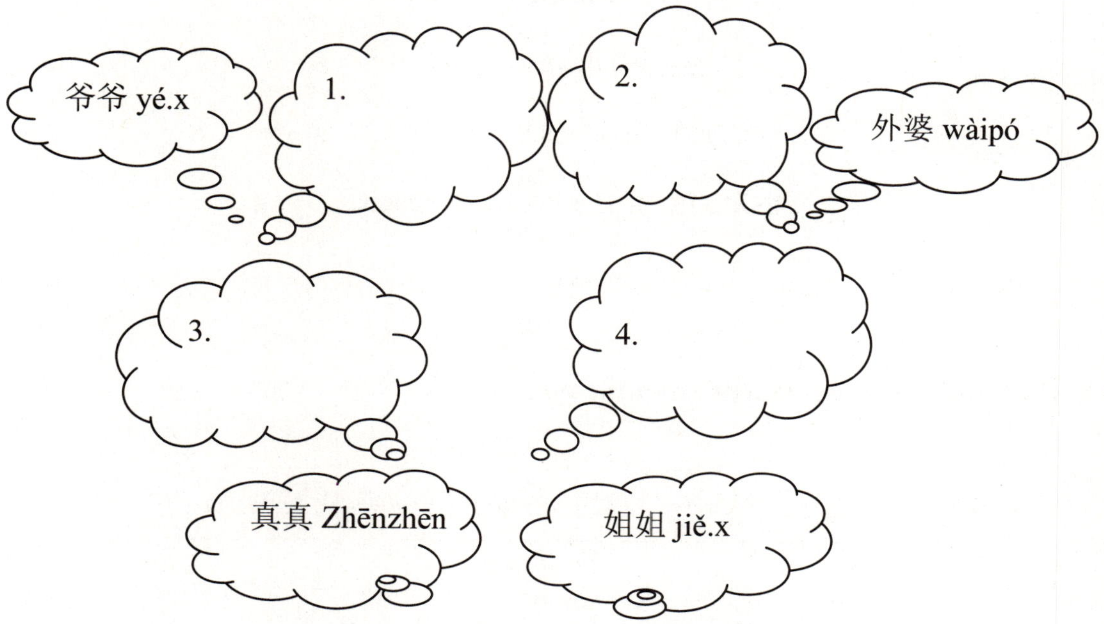

1. 真真有爷爷奶奶吗？ Zhēnzhēn yǒu yé.x nǎi.x .ma?

____

2. 真真家有几口人？ Zhēnzhēn jiā *yǒu jǐ*-kǒu rén?

____

3. 真真家有什么人？ Zhēnzhēn jiā yǒu shén.me rén?

____

名字：________________________ 日期：____________

2 Decide if 的 *.de* can be omitted in the following statements. Write an "O" if it can be omitted, or an "X" if it cannot be omitted.

1. ____________________ 我的朋友 wǒ.de péng.yǒu
2. ____________________ 他们的老师 tā.mén.de lǎoshī
3. ____________________ 我的兔子 wǒ.de tù.zi
4. ____________________ 你的妈妈 nǐ.de mā.x
5. ____________________ 白苹的生日 Bái Píng .de shēng.rì

3 Fill in the blanks with the words from the box.

叫 jiào	谁 shéi	哪 nǎ	我的 wǒ.de	爸爸妈妈 bà.x mā.x

1. ________________是你的中文老师 shì nǐ.de Zhōngwén lǎoshī？
2. ________________宠物是兔子 chǒngwù shì tù.zi。
3. 你的鸟 Nǐ.de niǎo________________什么名字 shén.me míng.zì？
4. 他们是你 Tā.mén shì nǐ________________吗.ma？
5. 你是 Nǐ shì________________国人 guó rén？

4 The underlined part is unknown. Change the following sentences into questions.

Li.zi: 她是我姐姐。Tā shì *wǒ* jiě.x.
谁是你姐姐？Shéi shì *nǐ* jiě.x?

1. 他们是我爸爸妈妈。Tā.mén shì wǒ bà.x mā.x.

____

2. 这个人是我哥哥。Zhèi-.ge rén shì wǒ gē.x.

____

3. 方老师是我的中文老师。Fāng lǎoshī shì wǒ.de Zhōngwén lǎoshī.

____

4. 那个人是我们的朋友。Nèi-.ge rén shì wǒ.mén.de péng.yǒu.

____

5. 我的猫叫胖胖。Wǒ.de māo jiào Pàngpàng.

____

6. 她的奶奶八十岁。Tā.de nǎi.x bā.shí-suì.

____

5 Unscramble the words or phrases to make complete sentences.

Lì.zi: 姐姐 jiě.x / 我 wǒ / 是 shì / 这 zhè
这是我姐姐 Zhè shì *wǒ* jiě.x。

1. 谁 shéi / 是 shì / 你们 nǐ.mén

____

2. 他们 tā .mén / 狗 gǒu / 小 xiǎo / 的.de / 很 hěn

____

3. 狗 gǒu / 的.de / 叫 jiào / 妹妹 mèi.x / 小可爱 *Xiǎo*kě'ài

____

4. 爸爸 bà.x / 是 shì / 我 wǒ / 这 zhè / 妈妈 mā.x

____

5. 是 shì / 宠物 chǒngwù / 的.de / 鱼 yú / 我 wǒ

____

6 Correct the following sentences.

Li.zi: 谁是这 Shéi shì zhè?
这是谁 Zhè shì shéi?

1. 这是他猫吗？Zhè shì tā māo .ma?

____

2. 谁是那个人？Shéi shì nèi-.ge rén?

____

3. 它的名字大可爱。Tā.de míng.zi Dàkě'ài.

____

4. 宠物是我的猫。Chǒngwù shì wǒ.de māo.

____

7 Match each sentence with the correct response from the box.

A. 对，那是我的狗 Duì, nà shì wǒ.de gǒu。
B. 不是，这是我哥哥 Bú.shì, zhè shì wǒ gē.x。
C. 那是我的老师 Nà shì wǒ.de lǎoshī。
D. 她是西班牙人 Tā shì Xībānyárén。

1. ________ 那是谁？Nà shì shéi?
2. ________ 那是你的宠物，对不对？Nà shì nǐ.de chǒngwù, duì .bú.duì?
3. ________ 谁是西班牙人？Shéi shì Xībānyárén?
4. ________ 这是你爸爸吗？Zhè shì nǐ bà.x .ma?

8 Answer the following questions.

1. 你的爸爸妈妈多大？Nǐ.de bà.x mā.x duó dà?

____

2. 你有宠物吗？*Nǐ yǒu* chǒngwù .ma? 它叫什么名字？Tā jiào shén.me míng.zì?

____

3. 你喜欢鸟吗？*Nǐ* xǐ.huān niǎo .ma?

____

4. 你的爷爷、奶奶多大年纪？Nǐ.de yé.x nǎi.x duó dà niánjì?

____

5. 你的外公、外婆叫什么名字？Nǐ .de wàigōng wàipó jiào shén.me míng.zì?

____

9 Fill in the blanks based on what you learned from the Culture Window.

1. The most welcomed pets for Chinese people are ____________ and ____________.

2. The top three most common pets in ancient China were ____________, ____________ and ____________.

3. In ancient China, horses were not kept as companions, but used for ____________, and koi fish for symbolizing ____________ in the family.

10 Create a family tree for your family or a famous family.

名字：________________________ 日期：____________

11 **Write a small paragraph in Pinyin to describe your family. You can use the presentation you did for Activity 16 in the textbook.**

Unit 2 Lesson B

1 Write the number and correct measure word in Chinese for the item or items.

Li.zi:

一 yí ， 个.ge

1.

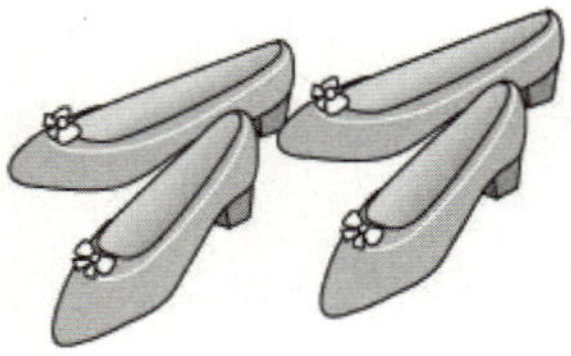

________ ， ________

4.

________ ， ________

7.

________ ， ________

2.

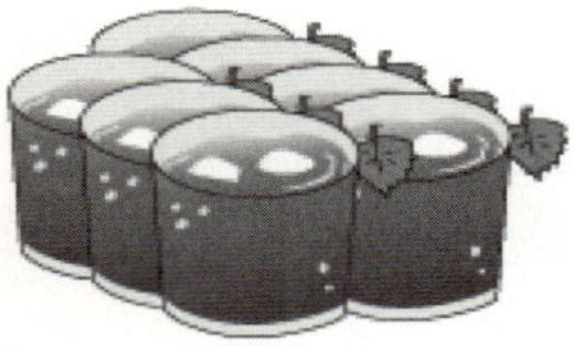

________ ， ________

5.

________ ， ________

8.

________ ， ________

3.

________ ， ________

6.

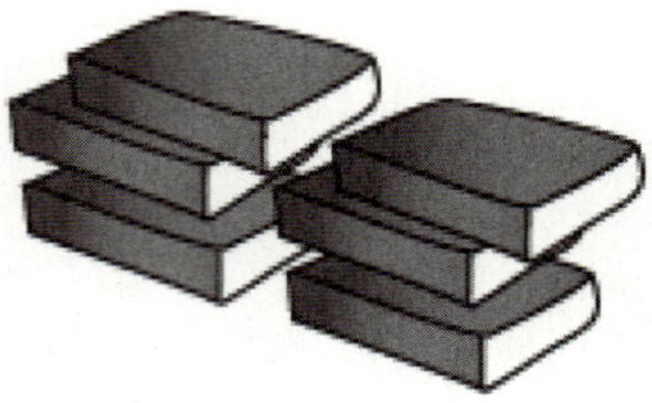

________ ， ________

9.

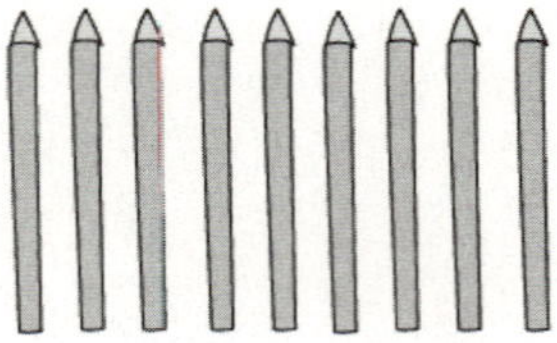

________ ， ________

2 Fill in the blanks with the words from the box.

和 hé	口 kǒu	两 liǎng	几 jǐ
可是 kě.shì	照片 zhàopiàn	没有 méi.yǒu	什么 shén.me

1. 我有 *Wǒ* yǒu______________个妹妹.ge mèi.x ，一个弟弟 yí-.ge dì.x。
2. 你有 *Nǐ yǒu*______________只乌龟 zhī wūguī？
3. 你家有几 Nǐ jiā *yǒu* jǐ______________人 rén？
4. 我是独生女 Wǒ shì dúshēngnǚ，我 wǒ______________兄弟姐妹 xiōngdì-jiěmèi。
5. 你有你奶奶的 *Nǐ yǒu nǐ* nǎi.x .de______________吗.ma？
6. 我家有我爸爸 Wǒ jiā *yǒu* wǒ bà.x、妈妈 mā.x、哥哥 gē.x，______________我 wǒ。
7. 我有外公 *Wǒ* yǒu wàigōng，______________我没有外婆 wǒ méi.yǒu wàipó。
8. 他家有 Tā jiā yǒu ______________人 rén？

3 Choose the correct answers to complete the dialogue.

1. ____ **A:** 你有几个兄弟姐妹？*Nǐ yǒu* jǐ-.ge xiōngdì-jiěmèi?

   B: a. 我是独生子。Wǒ shì dúshēngzǐ.

   b. 我没有弟弟。Wǒ méi.yǒu dì.x.

   c. 我家有四口人。Wǒ jiā yǒu sì-kǒu rén.

2. ____ **A:** 你家有几口人？Nǐ jiā yǒu *jǐ*-kǒu rén?

   B: a. 我没有弟弟。Wǒ méi.yǒu dì.x.

   b. 我家有三口人。Wǒ jiā yǒu sān-kǒu rén.

   c. 我家有爸爸、妈妈、姐姐，和我。Wǒ jiā yǒu bà.x, mā.x, jiě.x, hé wǒ.

3. ____ **A:** 你有宠物吗？*Nǐ yǒu* chǒngwù .ma?

B: a. 我没有兔子。Wǒ méi.yǒu tù.zi.

b. 我没有宠物。Wǒ méi.*yǒu* chǒngwù.

c. 我有狗和猫。*Wǒ yǒu* gǒu hé māo.

4. ____ **A:** 你有哥哥吗？*Nǐ* yǒu gē.x .ma?

B: a. 我没有姐姐。Wǒ méi.*yǒu* jiě.x.

b. 我有兄弟姐妹。*Wǒ* yǒu xiōngdì-jiěmèi.

c. 我没有哥哥，可是我有姐姐。Wǒ méi.yǒu gē.x, kě.shì *wǒ yǒu* jiě.x.

5. ____ **A:** 你有笔吗？*Nǐ yǒu* bǐ .ma?

B: a. 我没有笔。Wǒ méi.yǒu bǐ.

b. 我也没有纸。*Wǒ* yě méi.yǒu zhǐ.

c. 我也没有笔。*Wǒ* yě méi.yǒu bǐ.

4 Complete the dialogues according to the picture.

名字：________________________ 日期：__________

5 Correct each sentence.

Lì.zi: 我不有宠物。 Wǒ bù *yǒu* chǒngwù.
我没有宠物。 Wǒ méi.*yǒu* chǒngwù.

1. 你家有什么口人？ Nǐ jiā yǒu shén.me kǒu rén?

____

2. 我有七只书。 *Wǒ* yǒu qī-zhī shū .

____

3. 可是我有哥哥，我没有姐姐。 Kě.shì *wǒ* yǒu gē.x, wǒ méi.*yǒu* jiě.x.

____

4. 什么人你家有？ Shén.me rén nǐ jiā yǒu?

____

5. 他们家有二个猫。 Tā.mén jiā *yǒu* liǎng-.ge māo.

____

6. 我有三枝笔，和我也有三张纸。 *Wǒ* yǒu sān-zhī bǐ, hé *wǒ yě* yǒu sān-zhāng zhǐ.

____

6 Unscramble the words or phrases to make complete sentences.

Lì.zi: 姐姐 jiě.x / 我 wǒ / 是 shì / 这 zhè
这是我姐姐。Zhè shì *wǒ* jiě.x.

1. 你 nǐ / 这 zhè / 吗.ma / 鞋子 xié.zi / 是 shì / 的.de

____

2. 只 zhī / 两 liǎng / 有 yǒu / 我 wǒ / 猫 māo

____

3. 吗.ma / 你的 nǐ.de / 家人 jiārén / 他们 tā.mén / 是 shì

____

7 Fill in the blanks based on what you learned from the Culture Window.

1. For family members of the same generation on the mother's side or children of one's father's sisters, the word ______________ is added to the word that describes a sibling. For children of one's father's brothers, the word ______________ is added.

2. Sons of a brother are known as ______________ and nieces are ______________. Sons of a person's sister are ______________ and daughters of a person's sister are ______________.

名字：______________________ 日期：__________

8 Answer the following questions in Pinyin based on your own situation.

1. 你家有几口人 Nǐ jiā *yǒu jǐ*-kǒu rén？

   ____

2. 你家有什么人 Nǐ jiā yǒu shén.me rén？

   ____

3. 你是独生子 Nǐ shì dúshēngzǐ / 独生女吗 dúshēngnǚ .ma？

   ____

4. 你有几个兄弟姐妹 *Nǐ yǒu* jǐ-.ge xiōngdì-jiěmèi？

   ____

5. 你有几本中文书 *Nǐ yǒu jǐ*-běn Zhōngwén shū？

   ____

名字：_______________ 日期：_______________

Unit 2 Lesson C

1 **Write the date shown on each calendar on the line. Follow the model.**

Lì.zi:

八月十二号 Bāyuè shí'èr hào

1.______________ 3.______________ 5.______________

2.______________ 4.______________ 6.______________

名字：______________________ 日期：__________

2 Write the following telephone numbers in Arabic numbers. Follow the model.

	名字	电话号码	
	Lily	一三零七八九四六五三八 yī sān líng qī bā jiǔ sì liù wǔ sān bā	Li.zi: 130-789-46538
1.	Andy	一三九五七八一二三五六 yī sān *jiǔ* wǔ qī bā yī èr sān wǔ liù	
2.	Nora	一五九二二七六三五九八 yī *wǔ* jiǔ èr èr qī liù sān *wǔ* jiǔ bā	
3.	Mickey	一三一四三六七零三五六 yī sān yī sì sān liù qī líng sān wǔ liù	
4.	Edie	一三七六四八七二一零五 yī sān qī liù sì bā qī èr yī líng wǔ	
5.	Bob	一三四七五二九六零零八 yī sān sì qī wǔ èr jiǔ liù líng líng bā	

3 Fill in the blanks with the numbers in Chinese characters to complete the sequences.

1. 二十一 èr.shíyī，______________，二十三 èr.shísān，二十四 èr.shísì，______________，______________，______________。

2. 四 sì，______________，______________，______________，四十四 sì.shísì，五十四 wǔ.shísì，六十四 liù.shísì。

3. 九十一 jiǔ.shíyī，_______________，九十五 jiǔ.shíwǔ，_______________，

_______________，_______________。

4. 五十四 wǔ.shísì，_______________，_______________，_______________，

五十八 wǔ.shíbā，五十九 wǔ.shíjiǔ。

5. 七十三 qī.shísān，_______________，八十一 bā.shíyī，八十五 bā.shíwǔ，_______________，

_______________，九十七 jiǔ.shíqī。

6. 六十六 liù.shíliù，_______________，七十二 qī.shí’èr，_______________，

_______________，_______________。

4 Match each sentence below with the correct response from the box.

A. 不是。bú shì .	D. 三十号。sān.shí-hào.
B. 十二月。Shí’èryuè.	E. 八月十九日。Bāyuè shíjiǔ rì.
C. 我没有。Wǒ méi.yǒu .	F. 我也有手机。*Wǒ yě yǒu* shǒujī.

1. _____ 今天几号？ Jīn.tiān jǐ-hào?
2. _____ 这个月是几月？ Zhèi-.ge yuè shì jǐ-yuè?
3. _____ 我有手机，你呢？ Wǒ yǒu shǒujī, nǐ .ne?
4. _____ 这是你的手机吗？ Zhè shì nǐ.de shǒujī .ma?
5. _____ 他的生日是几月几日？ Tā.de shēng.rì shì jǐ-yuè jǐ-rì?
6. _____ 你有他的电话号码吗？ Nǐ yǒu tā.de diànhuà hàomǎ .ma?

5 Answer the questions according to the picture.

1. 他几岁？Tā jǐ-suì?

____

2. 他的生日是几月几号？Tā.de shēng.rì shì jǐ-yuè jǐ-hào?

____

3. 他有几张卡片？Tā *yǒu* jǐ-zhāng kǎpiàn?

____

4. 他有几个礼物？Tā *yǒu* jǐ-.ge lǐwù?

____

名字：______________________ 日期：__________

6 **Write the names of your favorite eight singers or bands on the lines below. Next to the blanks are the dates that the singers or bands will appear at the radio station. Write their names on your calendar.**

____________ 二月十五号 Èryuè shíwǔ hào

____________ 二月六号 Èryuè liù hào

____________ 二月二十八号 Èryuè èr.shíbā hào

____________ 二月十号 Èryuè shí hào

____________ 二月十九号 Èryuè shíjiǔ hào

____________ 二月三号 Èryuè sān hào

____________ 二月十一号 Èryuè shíyī hào

____________ 二月二十四号 Èryuè èr.shísì hào

Your Calendar

星期一 Xīngqīyī	星期二 Xīngqī'èr	星期三 Xīngqīsān	星期四 Xīngqīsì	星期五 Xīngqīwǔ	星期六 Xīngqīliù	星期日 Xīngqīrì
1	2	3	4	5	6	7
8	9	10	11	12	13	14
15	16	17	18	19	20	21
22	23	24	25	26	27	28

7 Write the corresponding question to each answer given.

1. **Q:** ______________________________

   A: 董太太的生日是一月一号。Dǒng tài.x .de shēng.rì shì Yīyuè yī hào.

2. **Q:** ______________________________

   A: 我的电话号码是 5798632。Wǒ.de diànhuà hàomǎ shì wǔ qī jiǔ bā liù sān èr.

3. **Q:** ______________________________

   A: 我有手机。*Wǒ yǒu* shǒujī.

4. **Q:** ______________________________

   A: 她的手机号码是 098652898。Tā.de shǒujī hàomǎ shì líng jiǔ bā liù wǔ èr bā jiǔ bā.

8 Fill in the blanks based on what you learned from the Culture Window.

1. The most important birthday is the child's ______________ birthday.
2. In the event 抓周 *zhuāzhōu*, if a child grabs an abacus, it means he or she may become a successful ______________.
3. China's cell phone numbers are composed of ______________ digits.

名字：________________ 日期：________

9 Answer the following questions.

1. 今天是几月几号？Jīn.tiān shì jǐ-yuè jǐ-hào?

____

2. 你的生日是几月几号？Nǐ.de shēng.rì shì jǐ-yuè jǐ-hào?

____

3. 万圣节是几月几号？Wànshèngjié shì jǐ-yuè jǐ-hào?

____

4. 圣诞节是几月几号？Shèngdànjié shì jǐ-yuè jǐ-hào?

____

5. 你有手机吗？*Nǐ yǒu* shǒujī .ma?

____

6. 你的电话号码是多少？Nǐ.de diànhuà hàomǎ shì duōshǎo?

____

Unit 2 Lesson D

1 **Draw a line from each activity to its corresponding picture.**

 1.	冰球 bīngqiú 滑板 huábǎn 棒球 bàngqiú 篮球 lánqiú 排球 páiqiú 游泳 yóuyǒng 足球 zúqiú 电子游戏 diànzǐ yóuxì	 5.
 2.		 6.
 3.		 7.
 4.		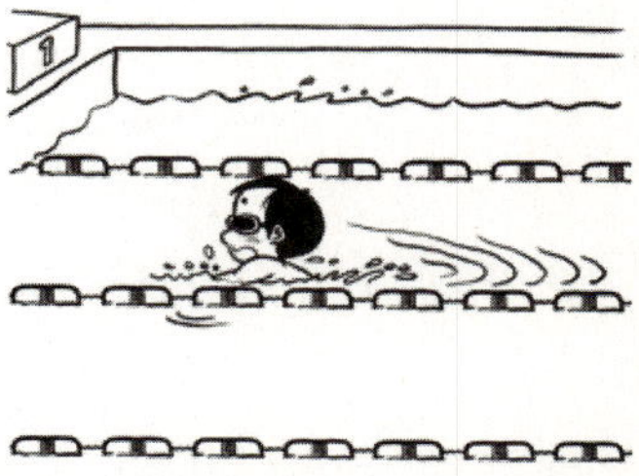 8.

2 **Fill in the blanks with the correct verbs for each activity.**

1. ______________ 饭 fàn
2. ______________ 书 shū
3. ______________ 歌 gē
4. ______________ 舞 wǔ
5. ______________ 字 zì
6. ______________ 话 huà
7. ______________ 泳 yǒng
8. ______________ 街 jiē
9. ______________ 画 huà
10. ______________ 网 wǎng
11. ______________ 足球 zúqiú
12. ______________ 排球 páiqiú
13. ______________ 滑板 huábǎn
14. ______________ 电影 diànyǐng
15. ______________ 音乐 yīnyuè
16. ______________ 电子游戏 diànzǐ yóuxì

3 **How would you answer the question 你喜欢做什么 *Nǐ xǐ.huān zuò shén.me*？ Choose your top five favorite activities from the previous activity to complete the following sentences.**

1. 我喜欢 *Wǒ* xǐ.huān ________________________________。
2. 我喜欢 *Wǒ* xǐ.huān ________________________________。
3. 我喜欢 *Wǒ* xǐ.huān ________________________________。
4. 我喜欢 *Wǒ* xǐ.huān ________________________________。
5. 我喜欢 *Wǒ* xǐ.huān ________________________________。

4 Use the pattern *V* 不 *bù/bú V* to rewrite the following questions.

Lì.zi: 姐姐听音乐吗？Jiě.x tīng-yīnyuè .ma？
姐姐听不听音乐？Jiě.x tīng .bù .tīng yīnyuè？

1. 她是德国人吗？Tā shì Dé.guórén .ma?

____

2. 你逛街吗？*Nǐ* guàngjiē .ma?

____

3. 他们打篮球吗？Tā.mén dǎ-lánqiú .ma?

____

4. 爸爸看法国电影吗？Bà.x kàn Fǎ.guó diànyǐng .ma?

____

5. 她们喜欢画画吗？Tā.mén xǐ.huān huà.x .ma?

____

6. 哥哥看中文书吗？Gē.x kàn Zhōngwén shū .ma?

____

7. 林老师说英文吗？Lín lǎoshī shuō Yīngwén .ma?

____

8. 你的生日是一月八号吗？Nǐ.de shēng.rì shì Yīyuè bā hào .ma?

____

5 Your friends don't know what you can do together tomorrow. Give each of them a suggestion with the hints provided and the particle 吧 *.ba.*

Lì.zi: Lydia (看电影 kàn-diànyǐng)
我们一起看电影吧！ Wǒ.mén yìqǐ kàn-diànyǐng .ba！

1. Aaron (踢足球 tī-zúqiú)

You: ____

2. Judy (逛街 guàngjiē)

You: ____

3. George (玩滑板 wán-huábǎn)

You: ____

名字：______________________ 日期：__________

6 This is the Chinese classroom bulletin board. Read the descriptions and answer the questions.

李小红 *Lǐ* Xiǎohóng	杨凡 Yáng Fán	林文 Lín Wén	张英英 Zhāng Yīngyīng
我喜欢逛街、跳舞 *Wǒ* xǐ.huān guàng-jiē, tiào-wǔ。 	我喜欢看书、打棒球 *Wǒ* xǐ.huān kàn-shū, dǎ-bàngqiú。 	我喜欢逛街、画画 *Wǒ* xǐ.huān guàng-jiē, huà.x。 	我喜欢唱歌、打篮球 *Wǒ* xǐ.huān chàng-gē, dǎ-lánqiú。 

1. If you like sports, who can you hang out with?

____

2. If you want to go shopping, who can you go with?

____

7 Fill in the blanks based on what you learned from the Culture Window.

1. The ________________ people introduced basketball to the Chinese in 1894.
2. Yao Ming, Wang Zhizhi and Mengke Bateer were called "The Walking ________________" at the Sydney Summer Olympics in 2000.
3. ________________ is the first Chinese player to play in the NBA.

名字：______________________ 日期：__________

8 Answer the following questions.

1. 你喜欢唱歌吗？*Nǐ* xǐ.huān chàng-gē .ma?

____

2. 你听不听音乐？Nǐ tīng .bù .tīng yīnyuè?

____

3. 你喜欢看电影吧？*Nǐ* xǐ.huān kàn-diànyǐng .ba?

____

4. 你的兄弟姐妹喜欢做什么？Nǐ.de xiōngdì-jiěmèi xǐ.huān zuò shén.me?

____

5. 你明天打不打篮球？Nǐ míng.tiān dǎ .bù .dǎ lánqiú?

____

6. 你爸妈说不说中文？Nǐ bàmā shuō .bù .shuō Zhōngwén?

____

名字：____________________ 日期：____________

Unit 3 Lesson A

1 Fill in the blanks with the appropriate location word from the box.

中间 zhōngjiān　右边 yòu.biān　左边 zuǒ.biān

2 Look at the arrows on the chair and fill in the location words from the box.

右边 yòu.biān	后面 hòu.miàn	下面 xià.miàn
前面 qián.miàn	上面 shàng.miàn	左边 zuǒ.biān

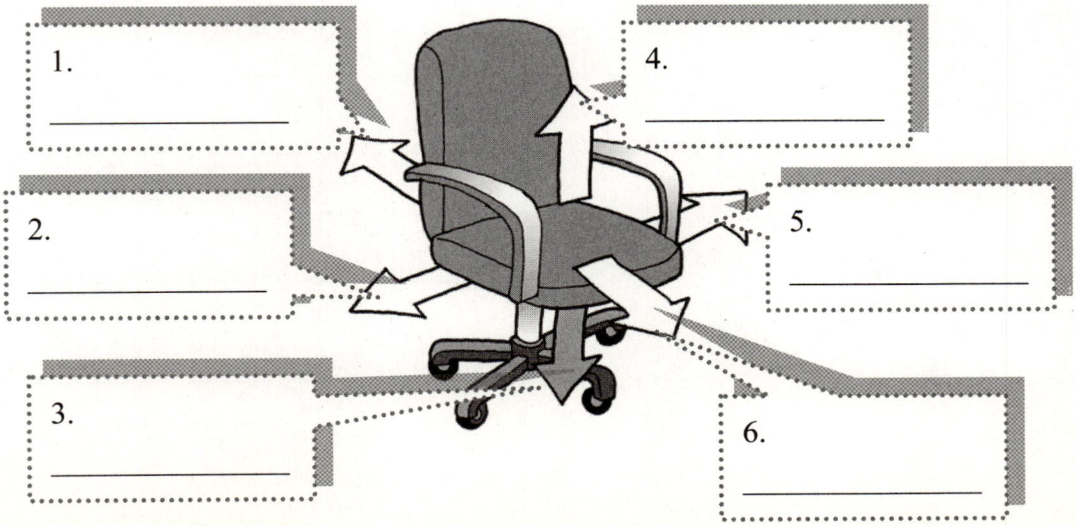

3 Look at the pictures and decide if each statement is true or false. Correct any false statements.

	**Lì.zi:** __F__ 书在背包前面。Shū zài bēibāo qián.miàn. 书在背包后面。Shū zài bēibāo hòu.miàn.
	_____ 1. 书在背包上面。Shū zài bēibāo shàng.miàn. ________________________________
	_____ 2. 书在背包下面。Shū zài bēibāo xià.miàn. ________________________________
	_____ 3. 书在背包外面。Shū zài bēibāo wài.miàn. ________________________________
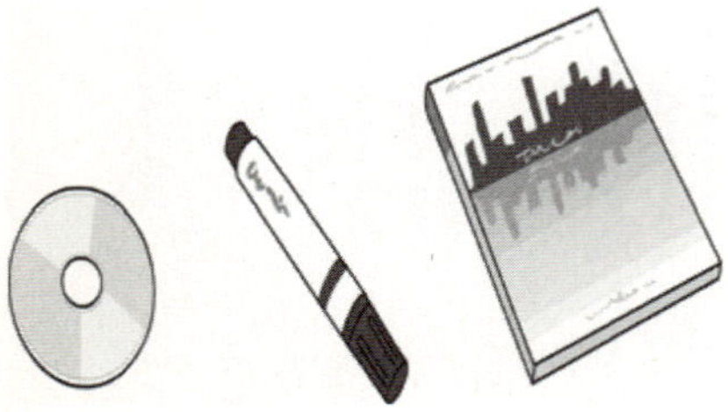	_____ 4. 书在光盘和白板笔中间 Shū zài guāngpán hé bái*bǎn*bǐ zhōngjiān。 ________________________________

名字：________________ 日期：________

4 Look at the picture and describe the locations of the following items.

Lì.zi: 讲台 jiǎngtái

讲台在教室前面。Jiǎngtái zài jiàoshì qián.miàn.

OR 讲台在老师和学生中间。Jiǎngtái zài lǎoshī hé xué.shēng zhōngjiān.

讲台在投影机下面。Jiǎngtái zài tóuyǐngjī xià.miàn.

1. 地图 dìtú：________________
2. 海报 hǎibào：________________
3. 板擦 bǎncā：________________
4. 光盘 guāngpán：________________
5. 背包 bēibāo：________________
6. 老师 lǎoshī：________________
7. 学生 xué.shēng：________________
8. 课本 kèběn：________________
9. 电脑 diànnǎo：________________
10. 桌子 zhuō.zi：________________
11. 投影机 tóuyǐngjī：________________
12. 白板笔 bái*bǎn*bǐ：________________
13. CD 播放机 CD bōfàngjī：________________

5 Look at the family photo and answer the following questions.

1. 爷爷在奶奶和爸爸中间吗？Yé.x zài nǎi.x hé bà.x zhōngjiān .ma?

____

2. 谁在妹妹后面？Shéi zài mèi.x hòu.miàn?

____

3. 爷爷前面是谁？Yé.x qián.miàn shì shéi?

____

4. 奶奶在哪儿？Nǎi.x zài nǎr?

____

5. 哥哥旁边是什么？Gē.x páng.biān shì shén.me?

____

6 Choose the best answer to each question.

1. _____ What are the two basic types of cram schools?

   A. talent and academic B. sports and academic C. talent and sports

2. _____ Compared to traditional schools, how is the atmosphere in talent schools?

   A. competitive B. lively C. casual

3. _____ Toward whom are language schools targeted?

   A. junior and senior high students B. children and adults

   C. people of all ages

7 Answer the following questions.

1. 你的背包在哪儿？Nǐ.de bēibāo zài nǎr? (when you are in class)

____

2. 你家前面有篮球场吗？Nǐ jiā qián.miàn yǒu lánqiúchǎng .ma?

____

3. 你家旁边是公园(*park*)吗？Nǐ jiā páng.biān shì gōngyuán .ma?

____

4. 在中文教室里，谁在你左边？谁在你右边？
   Zài Zhōngwén jiàoshì lǐ, shéi zài *nǐ* zuǒ.biān? Shéi zài nǐ yòu.biān?

____

名字：_______________ 日期：_______________

Unit 3 Lesson B

1 Write the time in Chinese characters and Pinyin. Follow the model.

Li.zi:

早上 zǎo.shàng

七点三十分 qī-diǎn sān.shí-fēn

1.

2.

3.

4.

5.

6.

2 Fill in the blanks with words from the box below.

在 zài	半 bàn	还 hái	刻 kè	点 diǎn	给 gěi	能 néng	一起 yìqǐ

1. 现在几 Xiànzài jǐ ________________？
2. 你的背包 Nǐ.de bēibāo ________________家里吗 jiālǐ .ma？
3. 他借篮球 Tā jiè lánqiú ________________他的同学 tā.de tóngxué。
4. 哥哥后天不 Gē.x hòu.tiān bù ________________去海边 qù hǎibiān。
5. 我要铅笔 Wǒ yào qiānbǐ，________________要圆珠笔 yào yuánzhūbǐ。
6. 周末我跟朋友 Zhōumò wǒ gēn péng.yǒu ________________看电影 kàn-diànyǐng。
7. 六点一 Liù-diǎn yī ________________是六点十五分 shì liù-diǎn shíwǔ-fēn。
8. 十一点 Shíyī-diǎn ________________是十一点三十分 shì shíyī-diǎn sān.shí-fēn。

3 Match the question on the left with the corresponding reply on the right.

1. ____ 谢谢你。Xiè.x nǐ.
2. ____ 现在几点？Xiànzài jǐ-diǎn?
3. ____ 他几点打球？Tā jǐ-diǎn dǎ-qiú?
4. ____ 给他们两张纸，好吗？
   Gěi tā.mén liǎng-zhāng zhǐ, hǎo .ma?
5. ____ 我们可以一起看书吗？
   Wǒ.mén kěyǐ yìqǐ kàn-shū .ma?
6. ____ 你不能给我课本，对不对？
   Nǐ bù néng gěi wǒ kèběn, duì .bú .duì?

A. 对。Duì.
B. 不客气。Bú kè.qì.
C. 两点半。Liǎng-diǎn bàn.
D. 当然可以。Dāngrán kěyǐ.
E. 我没有纸。Wǒ méi.yǒu zhǐ.
F. 现在十二点。Xiànzài shí'èr-diǎn.

4 Look at Li Wen's spring break schedule and answer the questions.

星期一	星期二	星期三	星期四	星期五
9:00 上中文课 shàng Zhōngwén kè	8:00 上英文课 shàng Yīngwén kè	10:30 画画 huà.x	10:00 上中文课 shàng Zhōngwén kè	9:30 借电脑给小华 jiè diànnǎo *gěi* Xiǎohuá
14:30 踢足球 tī-zúqiú	10:00 上网 shàngwǎng	16:40 跟哥哥打篮球 gēn gē.x dǎ -lánqiú	12:00 去海边游泳 qù hǎibiān yóuyǒng	16:15 踢足球 tī-zúqiú
18:00 跟奶奶吃饭 gēn nǎi.x chī-fàn	16:25 图书馆看书 túshūguǎn kàn-shū	19:00 看电影 kàn-diànyǐng	15:50 玩滑板 wán-huábǎn	19:00 玩电子游戏 wán-diànzǐ yóuxì

1. ____ 李文星期几上中文课？Lǐ Wén xīngqī-jǐ shàng Zhōngwén kè?
   A. 星期一、星期二 Xīngqīyī, Xīngqīèr
   B. 星期一、星期四 Xīngqīyī, Xīngqīsì
   C. 星期二、星期四 Xīngqī'èr, Xīngqīsì

2. ____ 李文星期二下午去哪儿？Lǐ Wén Xīngqī'èr xià.wǔ qù nǎr?
   A. 海边 hǎibiān
   B. 篮球场 lánqiúchǎng
   C. 图书馆 túshūguǎn

3. ____ 李文星期五晚上做什么？Lǐ Wén Xīngqī*wǔ* wǎn.shàng zuò shén.me?
   A. 玩滑板 wá-huábǎn
   B. 看电影 kàn-diànyǐng
   C. 玩电子游戏 wán-diànzǐ yóuxì

4. ____ 李文借什么给小华？Lǐ Wén jiè shén.me *gěi* Xiǎohuá?
   A. 电脑 diànnǎo
   B. 足球 zúqiú
   C. 篮球 lánqiú

5. ____ 李文几点上英文课？Lǐ Wén *jǐ*-diǎn shàng Yīngwén kè?
   A. 八点 bā-diǎn
   B. 九点 *jiǔ*-diǎn
   C. 十点 shí-diǎn

6. ____ 李文星期三上午做什么？Lǐ Wén Xīngqīsān shàngwǔ zuò shén.me?
   A. 画画 huà.x
   B. 打球 dǎ-qiú
   C. 看书 kàn-shū

7. ____ 李文星期四中午在哪儿？Lǐ Wén Xīngqīsì zhōngwǔ zài nǎr?
   A. 海边 hǎibiān
   B. 学校 xuéxiào
   C. 家里 jiālǐ

8. ____ 李文星期一晚上跟谁吃饭？Lǐ Wén Xīngqīyī wǎn.shàng gēn shéi chī-fàn?
   A. 奶奶 nǎi.x
   B. 哥哥 gē.x
   C. 小华 Xiǎohuá

5 Choose the best answer to each question.

1. ____ What are the four treasures of the study?

   A. ink, inkstone, paper, and teacher   B. brush, paper, book, and teacher
   C. brush, ink, paper, and inkstone

2. ____ Calligraphy has played an important role in which two fields?

A. art and literature B. literature and politics C. art and economy

3. ____ For using the four treasures of the study, which of the following statements is correct?

A. Hairs of the brush need to be bent to absorb more ink.
B. As with the brush, the inkstone also needs to be washed.
C. After using the four treasures, it is better to dry them under the sun.

6 Use the words provided to make sentences with the verb 借 *jiè*. There are two correct ways to make these sentences. Write both of them.

Lì.zi: 哥哥 gē.x / 弟弟 dì.x / 数学课本 shùxué kèběn
哥哥借给弟弟数学课本。Gē.x jiègěi dì.x shùxué kèběn.
哥哥借数学课本给弟弟。Gē.x jiè shùxué kè*běn* gěi dì.x.

1. 他 tā / 我 wǒ / 三张纸 sān-zhāng zhǐ

____

____

2. 国明 Guómíng / 林天 Líntiān / 笔记本 bǐjìběn

____

____

3. 王在军 Wáng Zàijūn / 他的同学 tā.de tóngxué / 他的电脑 tā.de diànnǎo

4. 李小姐 Lǐ *xiǎo*.jiě / 董先生 Dǒng xiān.shēng / CD 播放器 CD bōfàngqì

7 Answer the following questions.

1. 你明天可以打球吗？Nǐ míng.tiān *kěyǐ* dǎ-qiú .ma？

2. 你可以借给你的朋友你的电子游戏吗？
*Nǐ kě*yǐ jiè *gěi* nǐ.de péng.yǒu nǐ.de diànzǐ yóuxì .ma？

3. 你可以给你的同学你家的电话号码吗？
Nǐ kěyǐ gěi nǐ.de tóngxué nǐ jiā .de diànhuà hàomǎ .ma？

名字：______________________ 日期：__________

8 **What do you carry in your backpack to school? Make a list.**

Unit 3 Lesson C

1 Answer the questions below according to the illustrations in the chart.

英文课 Yīngwén kè	中文课 Zhōngwén kè	数学课 shùxué kè	体育课 tǐyù kè

1. 中文课难吗？Zhōngwén kè nán .ma?

____

2. 数学课容不容易？Shùxué kè róng .bù róngyì?

____

3. 体育课好不好玩儿？Tǐyù kè hǎo .bù hǎowánr?

____

4. 英文课有没有意思？Yīngwén kè yǒu .méi.yǒu yì.sī?

____

2 Look at the schedule and decide if each statement is true or false. Correct any false statements.

今天是星期三，这是李明的日历。Jīntiān shì Xīngqīsān, zhè shì Lǐ Míng .de rìlì.

Monday	Tuesday	Wednesday	Thursday	Friday
10:00 a.m. 历史小考 lìshǐ *xiǎo*kǎo	2:00 p.m. 打篮球 dǎ-lánqiú	8:00 a.m. 去健身房 qù jiànshēnfáng	4:00 p.m. 上中文课 shàng Zhōngwén kè	6:00 p.m. 去外婆家 qù wàipó jiā

1. 李明昨天下午三点打篮球。 Lǐ Míng zuótiān xià.wǔ sān-*diǎn* dǎ-lánqiú.

____

2. 李明后天晚上去奶奶家。 Lǐ Míng hòu.tiān wǎn.shàng qù nǎi.x jiā.

____

3. 李明这个星期有一个小考。 Lǐ Míng zhèi.ge xīngqī yǒu yí-.ge *xiǎo*kǎo.

____

4. 李明明天没有中文课。 Lǐ Míng míng.tiān méi.yǒu Zhōngwén kè.

____

5. 李明今天晚上去健身房。 Lǐ Míng jīn.tiān wǎn.shàng qù jiànshēnfáng.

____

3 Choose the correct answer.

1. ____ **A:** 今天是星期六，后天是星期几？
Jīn.tiān shì Xīngqīliù, hòu.tiān shì xīngqī jǐ?
B: a. 星期二 Xīngqī'èr
b. 星期一 Xīngqīyī
c. 星期四 Xīngqīsì

2. ____ **A:** 你觉得中文课难吗？Nǐ jué.de Zhōngwén kè nán .ma?
B: a. 我今天上中文课。Wǒ jīn.tiān shàng Zhōngwén kè.
b. 今天的中文小考很难。Jīn.tiān .de Zhōngwén *xiǎokǎo* hěn nán.
c. 我觉得很难，可是很有意思。Wǒ jué.de hěn nán, kě.shì *hěn* yǒu yì.sī.

3. ____ **A:** 你下星期一有考试吗？Nǐ xià Xīngqīyī *yǒu* kǎoshì .ma?
B: a. 考试很容易。Kǎoshì hěn róngyì.
b. 我不想考试。Wǒ bù *xiǎng* kǎoshì.
c. 我有三个小考。*Wǒ* yǒu sān-.ge *xiǎo*kǎo.

4. ____ **A:** 你星期几有数学课？Nǐ xīngqī-*jǐ* yǒu shùxué kè?
B: a. 我觉得数学课很有挑战性。
Wǒ jué.de shùxué kè *hěn yǒu* tiǎozhànxìng.
b. 我星期二和星期四有数学课。
Wǒ Xīngqī'èr hé Xīngqīsì yǒu shùxué kè.
c. 我星期三没有数学课。Wǒ Xīngqīsān méi.yǒu shùxué kè.

5. ____ **A:** 你明天下午去哪儿？Nǐ míng.tiān xià.wǔ qù nǎr?
B: a. 我得下午回家。*Wǒ* děi xià.wǔ huí-jiā.
b. 明天我不来学校。Míng.tiān wǒ bù lái xuéxiào.
c. 我得去图书馆借书。*Wǒ* děi qù túshūguǎn jièshū.

4 Use the adverb 还 *hái* to combine the two sentences.

1. 我有两个妹妹。我有一个弟弟。Wǒ yǒu liǎng-.ge mèi.x. Wǒ yǒu yí-.ge dì.x.

____

2. 他们昨天去健身房。他们昨天去电影院。
Tā.mén zuó.tiān qù jiànshēnfáng. Tā.mén zuó.tiān qù diànyǐngyuàn.

____

3. 奶奶有一只猫。奶奶有一只兔子。Nǎi.x yǒu yì-zhī māo. Nǎi.x yǒu yì-zhī tù.zi.

____

4. 我昨天有中文小考。我昨天有历史小考。
Wǒ zuó.tiān yǒu Zhōngwén xiǎokǎo. Wǒ zuótiān yǒu lìshǐ xiǎokǎo.

____

5. 弟弟喜欢打篮球。弟弟喜欢游泳。Dì.x xǐ.huān dǎ-lánqiú. Dì.x xǐ.huān yóuyǒng.

____

6. 我们星期日看中国电影。我们星期日看法国电影。
Wǒ.mén Xīngqīrì kàn Zhōng.guó diànyǐng. Wǒ.mén Xīngqīrì kàn Fǎ.guó diànyǐng.

____

5 Look at the following results of a survey on five school subjects. Answer the questions according to the chart.

	中文 Zhōngwén	历史 Lìshǐ	生物 Shēngwù	英文 Yīngwén	化学 Huàxué
难 nán	Mark, Isabelle		Mark	Ming, Frank	Ming
容易 róngyì	Ming	Isabelle	Roger, Frank	Zoe, Isabelle	
好玩儿 hǎowánr	Frank	Mark, Zoe		Roger	Isabelle
不好玩儿 bù hǎo wánr		Ming	Ming, Zoe		Roger
有挑战性 *yǒu* tiǎozhànxìng	Zoe, Roger	Roger	Isabelle		Zoe
无聊 wúliáo		Frank		Mark	Mark, Frank

1. Who finds the Chinese class challenging?

____

2. How many people think the chemistry class is boring?

____

3. Who likes history class? Who doesn't like history class?

____

4. Who thinks biology class is not fun?

____

名字：________________________ 日期：____________

6 Choose the best answer.

1. ____ At what time is the first period of class?

   A. 7:30 B. 8:00 C. 9:00

2. ____ For what class do Chinese students usually change the classroom?

   A. English B. Mathematics C. Music

3. ____ What do Chinese students usually do for homeroom?

   A. take tests B. talk to classmates C. clean the classroom

7 Answer the following questions.

1. 你星期五有几堂课？Nǐ Xīngqīwǔ *yǒu* jǐ-táng kè?

   ____

2. 你下个星期有考试吗？Nǐ xià.ge xīngqī *yǒu* kǎoshì .ma?

   ____

3. 你昨天上什么课？Nǐ zuó.tiān shàng shén.me kè?

   ____

4. 你星期几有中文课？Nǐ xīngqī-*jǐ* yǒu Zhōngwén kè?

   ____

名字：________________ 日期：________

Unit 3 Lesson D

1 Draw a line from each activity to its corresponding picture.

1.

2.

3.

4.

滑雪 huá-xuě

举重 jǔzhòng

台球 táiqiú

瑜珈 yújiā

慢跑 mànpǎo

网球 wǎngqiú

冲浪 chōnglàng

高尔夫 gāo’ěrfū

5.

6.

7.

8.

2 Fill in the blank with the correct verb for each activity.

1. _______________ 雪 xuě
2. _______________ 排球 páiqiú
3. _______________ 电视 diànshì
4. _______________ 瑜珈 yújiā
5. _______________ 台球 táiqiú
6. _______________ 自行车 zìxíngchē
7. _______________ 高尔夫 gāo'ěrfū
8. _______________ 有氧运动 *yǒu*yǎng yùndòng

3 Fill in the appropriate place word for each activity from the box below.

海边 hǎibiān	美术馆 měishùguǎn	篮球场 lánqiúchǎng
健身房 jiànshēnfáng	网球场 wǎngqiúchǎng	购物中心 gòuwù zhōngxīn
高尔夫球场 gāo'ěrfū qiúchǎng		

1. 我要去 Wǒ yào qù _________________________买东西 mǎi dōng.xī。
2. 他在 Tā zài _________________________打篮球 dǎ-lánqiú。
3. 你去 Nǐ qù _________________________看画吗 kàn huà .ma？
4. 他们星期六去 Tā.mén Xīngqīliù qù _________________________冲浪 chōnglàng。
5. 李小姐去 Lǐ *xiǎo*jiě qù _________________________做有氧运动 zuò *yǒu*yǎng yùndòng。
6. 他们要去 Tā.mén yào qù _________________________打网球吗 *dǎ*-wǎngqiú .ma？
7. 爷爷去 Yé.x qù _________________________打高尔夫 dǎ gāo'ěrfū。

名字：______________________ 日期：__________

4 Match each sentence with the correct response from the box.

A. 我去博物馆。Wǒ qù bówùguǎn.
B. 我周末也要去。Wǒ zhōumò yě yào qù.
C. 不，我要去购物中心。Bù, wǒ yào qù gòuwù zhōngxīn.
D. 对，我去那儿买背包。Duì, wǒ qù nàr mǎi bèibāo.
E. 周末快乐！Zhōumò kuàilè!

1. ______ 你要去博物馆吗？Nǐ yào qù bówùguǎn .ma?
2. ______ 明天是星期六！Míngtiān shì Xīngqīliù!
3. ______ 他周末要去海边游泳。Tā zhōumò yào qù hǎibiān yóuyǒng.
4. ______ 你星期五做什么？Nǐ Xīngqīwǔ zuò shén.me?
5. ______ 你去购物中心买东西吗？Nǐ qù gòuwù zhōngxīn mǎi dōng.xī .ma?

5 Choose the best response to complete the dialogue.

1. ______ **A:** 你要去网球场吗？Nǐ yào qù wǎngqiúchǎng .ma?

   B: a. 我来网球场。Wǒ lái wǎngqiúchǎng.

   b. 我不去网球场。Wǒ bú qù wǎngqiúchǎng.

   c. 我不喜欢打网球。Wǒ bù xǐ.huān *dǎ*-wǎngqiú.

2. ______ **A:** 他星期日要来我家，你呢？Tā Xīngqīrì yào lái wǒ jiā, nǐ .ne?

   B: a. 我不去他家。Wǒ bú qù tā jiā.

   b. 我也要去你家。*Wǒ* yě yào qù nǐ jiā.

   c. 我星期日不在他家。Wǒ Xīngqīrì bú zài tā jiā.

3. ______ **A:** 我周末要去滑雪，你周末要做什么？

Wǒ zhōumò yào qù huá-xuě, nǐ zhōumò yào zuò shén.me?

B: a. 我要去慢跑。Wǒ yào qù mànpǎo.

b. 我要跟你去打球。Wǒ yào gēn nǐ qù dǎ-qiú.

c. 我还要去爷爷家。Wǒ hái yào qù yé.x jiā.

4. ______ **A:** 你们星期六去哪儿？Nǐ.mén Xīngqīliù qù nǎr?

B: a. 我们不在家。Wǒ.mén bú zài jiā.

b. 我们去公园。Wǒ.mén qù gōngyuán.

c. 我们不去学校。Wǒ.mén bú qù xuéxiào.

5. ______ **A:** 他今天跟你们去美术馆吗？Tā jīn.tiān gēn nǐ.mén qù měishùguǎn .ma?

B: a. 对，他不去美术馆。Duì, tā bú qù měishùguǎn.

b. 对，我们一起去美术馆。Duì, wǒ.mén yìqǐ qù měishùguǎn.

c. 对，他们今天去美术馆。Duì, tā.mén jīn.tiān qù měishùguǎn.

6 Translate the following sentences using the preposition 跟 *gēn*.

1. Richard goes to the basketball court with Danny.

____

2. I go to the shopping center with my classmates today.

____

3. Grandmother watches television with her cats.

____

4. Grandfather played tennis with his friends yesterday afternoon.

____

5. My parents are having a meal with Mr. Lin this weekend.

____

6. He is going to the art museum with his father and brothers.

____

7 Change the following affirmative sentences to negative sentences. Follow the model.

Li.zi: 妈妈跟姐姐去购物中心。Mā.x gēn jiě.x qù gòuwù zhōngxīn.
妈妈不跟姐姐去购物中心。Mā.x bù gēn jiě.x qù gòuwù zhōngxīn.

1. 你们跟他们打台球。Nǐ.mén gēn tā.mén dǎ-táiqiú.

____

2. 哥哥跟弟弟玩电子游戏。Gē.x gēn dì.x wán-diànzǐ yóuxì.

____

3. 爸爸今天晚上跟我们吃饭。Bà.x jīntiān wǎnshàng gēn wǒ.mén chī-fàn.

____

4. 林华跟我一起去学校。Lín Huá gēn wǒ yìqǐ qù xuéxiào.

____

8 Choose the best answer.

1. ______ Which of the following statements is not true about parks in China?

A. People use parks as a place to work out in the morning.
B. Parks are a quiet place to do meditation.
C. Everyone enjoys talking with neighbors or friends in parks.

2. ______ Which of the following statements is true about night markets?

A. They only sells foods.
B. Red lanterns are the symbol of night markets.
C. Unusual snacks can be found at some night markets.

3. ______ What is not provided in a KTV?

A. songs B. foods C. movies

9 Answer the following questions.

1. 你周末要做什么？Nǐ zhōumò yào zuò shén.me?

____

2. 你昨天跟你的同学去图书馆吗？Nǐ zuó.tiān gēn nǐ.de tóngxué qù túshūguǎn .ma?

____

3. 你星期几去打篮球？Nǐ xīngqī-jǐ qù dǎ-lánqiú?

____

4. 你跟谁打篮球？Nǐ gēn shéi dǎ-lánqiú?

____

5. 你明天要去学校吗？Nǐ míng.tiān yào qù xuéxiào .ma?

____

6. 你同学星期五晚上要来你家吗？Nǐ tóngxué Xīngqī*wǔ* wǎn.shàng yào lái nǐ jiā .ma?

____

名字：______________________ 日期：__________

Unit 4 Lesson A

1 Fill in the correct answers according to the pictures.

1. **A:** 你好！请问你要点什么？

   Nǐ hǎo! Qǐngwèn nǐ yào diǎn shén.me?

   B: 我要一个 Wǒ yào yí-.ge ______________。

2. **A:** 你好！请问你要点什么？

   Nǐ hǎo! Qǐngwèn nǐ yào diǎn shén.me?

   B: 我要一个 Wǒ yào yí-.ge ______________。

3. **A:** 你好！请问你要点什么？

   Nǐ hǎo! Qǐngwèn nǐ yào diǎn shén.me?

   B: 我要一个 Wǒ yào yí-.ge ______________。

4. **A:** 你好！请问你要点什么？

   Nǐ hǎo! Qǐngwèn nǐ yào diǎn shén.me?

   B: 我要一个 Wǒ yào yí-.ge ______________。

5. **A:** 你好！请问你要点什么？

   Nǐ hǎo! Qǐngwèn nǐ yào diǎn shén.me?

   B: 我要一个 Wǒ yào yí-.ge ______________。

名字：________________ 日期：________

2 According to the answers, use 还是 *hái.shì* to ask the questions.

Li.zi: **A:** 你要吉士汉堡包还是三明治？

Nǐ yào jíshì hànbǎobāo háishì sānmíngzhì?

B: 我要三明治。Wǒ yào sānmíngzhì.

1. **A:** ________________________________?

   B: 小杯，谢谢。Xiǎo bēi, xiè.x.

2. **A:** ________________________________?

   B: 我和妈妈去快餐店。Wǒ hé mā.x qù kuàicān diàn.

3. **A:** ________________________________?

   B: 我要点大份的洋芋片。Wǒ yào diǎn dà fèn .de yángyùpiàn.

4. **A:** ________________________________?

   B: 汽水或果汁都可以。Qìshuǐ huò guǒzhī dōu kě.yǐ.

5. **A:** ________________________________?

   B: 我喜欢早上喝咖啡。Wǒ xǐ.huān zǎo.shàng hē kāfēi.

6. **A:** ________________________________?

   B: 我不喜欢游泳，可是我喜欢打网球。

   Wǒ bù xǐ.huān yóuyǒng, kě.shì wǒ xǐ.huān dǎ-wǎngqiú.

名字：________________ 日期：________

3 Use the words provided to make sentences with 一下 *yí.xià.*

Lì.zi: 我想看这本书。*Wǒ* xiǎng kàn zhèi-běn shū.
我想看一下这本书。*Wǒ* xiǎng kàn yí.xià zhèi-běn shū.

1. 我要看电视。Wǒ yào kàn-diànshì.

____

2. 哥哥想游泳。Gē.x xiǎng yóuyǒng.

____

3. 我得写作业。*Wǒ děi* xiě-zuòyè.

____

4. 姐姐想玩电子游戏。Jiě.x xiǎng wán diànzǐ yóuxì.

____

5. 你可以跟我去图书馆吗？*Nǐ kě*yǐ gēn wǒ qù túshūguǎn .ma?

____

4 **For questions 1 through 3, answer the questions. For questions 4 through 6, write the questions.**

1. **Q:** 你要茶还是咖啡？
   Nǐ yào chá hái.shì kāfēi?

   A: ____________________________。

2. **Q:** 你要果汁还是水？
   Nǐ yào guǒzhī hái.shì shuǐ?

   A: ____________________________。

3. **Q:** 你要汽水还是咖啡？
   Nǐ yào qìshuǐ hái.shì kāfēi?

   A: ____________________________。

4. **Q:** ____________________________?

   A: 我要水，谢谢。Wǒ yào shuǐ, xiè.x.

5. **Q:** ____________________________?

   A: 我要汽水。Wǒ yào qìshuǐ.

6. **Q:** ____________________________?

   A: 我要大杯。Wǒ yào dà bēi.

名字：______________________ 日期：__________

5 Decide if the following statements are true or false. Correct any false ones.

1. ______ The first fast food restaurant opened in China in 1990. Since then, the number of overweight children has increased.

____

2. ______ The Chinese government welcomes foreign food chain stores to open shops in famous historical sites such as Tiananmen Square and Beihai Park.

____

3. ______ The Beijing government grants licenses to chain convenience stores in a much slower way because it owns most of the traditional convenience stores.

____

6 Answer the following questions in Pinyin.

1. 你喜欢喝水还是饮料？ *Nǐ* xǐ.huān hē-shuǐ hái.shì yǐnliào?

____

2. 你喜欢快餐店的食物吗？ *Nǐ* xǐ.huān kuàicāndiàn .de shíwù .ma?

____

3. 你通常(*usually*)在快餐店点什么？ Nǐ tōngcháng zài kuàicāndiàn diǎn shén.me?

____

7 According to the list from a fast-food store below, connect each name to the corresponding food they order.

方先生 Fāng xiān.shēng	一个三明治 yí-.ge sānmíngzhì 一杯果汁 yì-bēi guǒzhī
吴先生 Wú xiān.shēng	四份热狗 sì-fèn règǒu
张小姐 Zhāng *xiǎo*.jiě	一份色拉 yí-fèn sèlā
白先生 Bái xiān.shēng	一份洋芋片 yí-fèn yángyùpiàn

1. _____ 方大同 Fāng Dàtóng

A. 

2. _____ 吴明 Wú Míng

B. 

3. _____ 张小妮 Zhāng Xiǎoní

C. 

4. _____ 白秋雨 Bái Qiūyǔ

D. 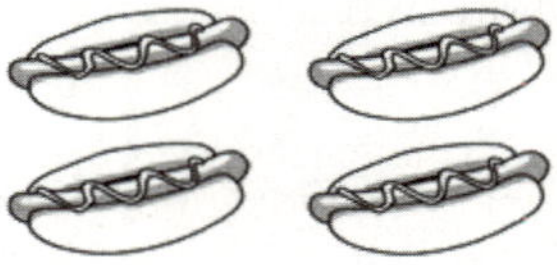

名字：________________ 日期：__________

8 **You work in a fast-food restaurant. Your co-worker is preparing meals for customers, but he made a few mistakes. Based on the meals prepared and the order list, decide if each customer gets what they ordered. If not, help your co-worker find the right meal.**

Meal one: 	Meal two: 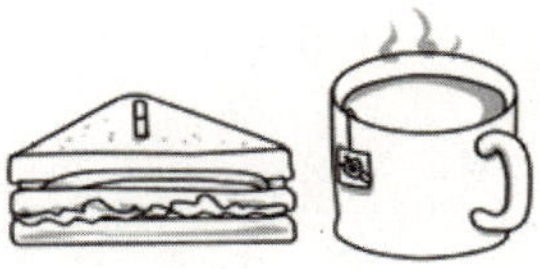	Meal three: 
Meal four: 	Meal five: 	Meal six: 

Customer A: 我要喝小杯的饮料，吃小份的东西。
Wǒ yào hē xiǎo bēi .de yǐnliào, chī xiǎo fèn .de dōng.xī.

Customer B: 我要喝大杯的饮料，吃大份的东西。
Wǒ yào hē dà bēi .de yǐnliào, chī dà fèn .de dōng.xī.

Customer C: 我只喝水，喜欢吃水果。*Wǒ* zhǐ hē-shuǐ, xǐ.huān chī *shuǐ*guǒ.

Customer D: 我要吃热狗和汉堡，我也喜欢喝汽水，但是我不喜欢吃薯条。 Wǒ yào chī règǒu hé hànbǎo, *wǒ yě* xǐhuān hē qìshuǐ, dànshì wǒ bù xǐ.huān chī shǔtiáo.

Customer E: 我想吃很多东西。*Wǒ* xiǎng chī hěn duō dōng.xī.

Customer F: 我要吃色拉，还要喝大杯果汁。Wǒ yào chī sèlā, hái yào hē dà bēi guǒzhī.

Match list your co-worker did	Right or Wrong?	The right Meal should be:
Customer A → Meal one	____________	____________
Customer B → Meal two	____________	____________
Customer C → Meal three	____________	____________
Customer D → Meal four	____________	____________
Customer E → Meal five	____________	____________
Customer F → Set six	____________	____________

名字：________________ 日期：________

Unit 4 Lesson B

1 **Draw a line from each quantity to its corresponding illustration, and fill in the Pinyin.**

一份	一杯	一壶	一罐	一瓶
________	________	________	________	________

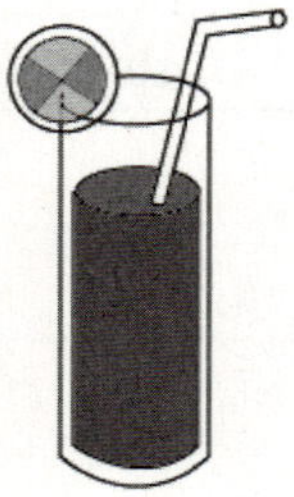

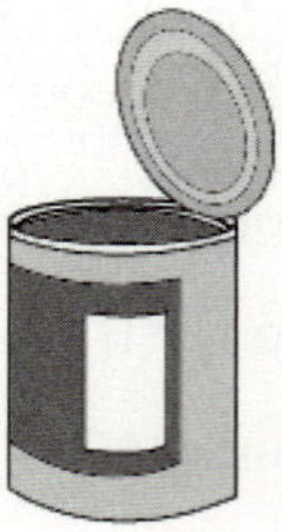

名字：______________________ 日期：__________

2 Fill in the blanks with the words in the box.

壶 hú	杯 bēi	请问 qǐngwèn	只 zhǐ	不用 búyòng	点 diǎn
份 fèn	对不起 duì.bùqǐ	有没有 yǒu .méi.yǒu	香草 xiāngcǎo		

1. **A:** 你要 Nǐ yào__________吃的东西吗 chī .de dōng.xī .ma？

   B: __________，谢谢 xiè.x。

2. **A:** __________，你们有热巧克力吗 nǐ.mén yǒu rè qiǎo.kèlì .ma？

   B: __________，我们没有热巧克力 wǒ.mén méi.yǒu rè qiǎo.kèlì。

3. **A:** 请问你要点什么喝的东西 Qǐngwèn nǐ yào diǎn shén.me hē .de dōng.xī？

   B: 我要一杯 Wǒ yào yì-bēi__________奶昔 nǎixī。

4. **A:** 请问你们 Qǐngwèn nǐ.mén__________吃的东西 chī .de dōng.xī？

   B: 对不起 Duì.bùqǐ，我们 wǒ.mén__________有饮料 *yǒu* yǐnliào。

5. **A:** 请问您要点什么 Qǐngwèn nín yào diǎn shén.me？

   B: 我要一 Wǒ yào yí__________三明治 sānmíngzhì，还要一

   hái yào yì__________橙汁 chéngzhī。

6. **A:** 你们要茶吗 Nǐ.mén yào chá .ma？

   B: 要 Yào，我们有两个人 Wǒ.mén *yǒu* liǎng-.ge rén，请给我们一 *qǐng gěi* wǒ.mén

   yì__________花茶 huāchá。

名字：______________________ 日期：__________

3 Choose the correct response to the questions that follow.

A. 对不起，我们没有冰沙。Duì.bùqǐ, wǒ.mén méiyǒu bīngshā.

B. 我要点吃的东西。Wǒ yào diǎn chī .de dōng.xī.

C. 我喜欢喝葡萄汁。*Wǒ* xǐ.huān hē pú.táozhī.

D. 要，请给我们一壶花茶。Yào, *qǐng gěi* wǒ.mén yì-hú huāchá.

E. 我们有热狗、薯条和三明治。Wǒ.mén yǒu règǒu, shǔtiáo hé sānmíngzhì.

F. 我们有红茶、绿茶、花茶，还有乌龙茶。

Wǒ.mén yǒu hóngchá, lǜchá, huāchá, hái yǒu wūlóngchá.

G. 我要巧克力奶昔。Wǒ yào qiǎo.kèlì nǎixī.

1. ______ 你们有什么茶？Nǐ.mén yǒu shén.me chá?

2. ______ 你喜欢喝什么果汁？*Nǐ* xǐ.huān hē shén.me guǒzhī?

3. ______ 请问你们要点喝的东西吗？Qǐngwèn nǐ.mén yào diǎn hē .de dōng.xī .ma?

4. ______ 你们有什么吃的东西？Nǐ.mén yǒu shén.me chī .de dōng.xī?

5. ______ 我要点喝的东西，你呢？Wǒ yào diǎn hē .de dōng.xī, nǐ .ne?

6. ______ 你们有没有冰沙？Nǐ.mén yǒu méi.yǒu bīngshā?

7. ______ 你要巧克力奶昔还是香草奶昔？Nǐ yào qiǎo.kèlì nǎixī hái.shì xiāng*cǎo* nǎixī?

名字：________________ 日期：________

4 Use 有没有 *yǒu méi.yǒu* to rewrite the sentences below.

Li.zi: 你有兄弟姐妹吗？*Nǐ* yǒu xiōngdì-jiěmèi .ma?
你有没有兄弟姐妹？*Nǐ* yǒu méi.yǒu xiōngdì-jiěmèi?

1. 你们有吃的东西吗？Nǐ.mén yǒu chī .de dōng.xī .ma?

____

2. 这个餐厅有花茶吗？Zhèi-.ge cāntīng yǒu huāchá .ma?

____

3. 他有中文书吗？Tā yǒu Zhōngwén shū .ma?

____

4. 这个学校有英国学生吗？Zhèi.-ge xuéxiào yǒu Yīng.guó xué.shēng .ma?

____

5. 背包里面有课本吗？Bēibāo lǐ.miàn yǒu kèběn .ma?

____

6. 那个快餐店有葡萄汁吗？Nèi.-ge kuàicāndiàn yǒu pú.táozhī .ma?

____

名字：________________ 日期：________

5 Look at the menu and answer the questions.

大大饮料店

红茶	￥3.00	汽水	￥6.00	奶昔	￥9.00
绿茶	￥3.00	橙汁	￥7.00	柠檬冰沙	￥18.00
乌龙茶	￥4.50	葡萄汁	￥8.00	奶香草昔	￥15.50
奶茶	￥5.50	咖啡	￥10.00	巧克力奶昔	￥15.00

1. 这个饮料店(*drink shop*)有什么果汁？Zhèi-.ge yǐnliào diàn yǒu shén.me guǒzhī?

____

2. 这个饮料店有没有花茶？Zhèi-.ge yǐnliào diàn yǒu méi.yǒu huāchá?

____

3. 你有五块钱，可以买什么饮料？*Nǐ yǒu* wǔ-kuài qián, *kěyǐ* mǎi shén.me yǐnliào?

____

4. 这个饮料店卖不卖吃的东西？Zhèi-.ge yǐnliào diàn mài bú mài chī .de dōng.xī?

____

5. 茶和果汁你都不喜欢，你可以点什么？
Chá hé guǒzhī nǐ dōu bù xǐ.huān, *nǐ kěyǐ* diǎn shén.me?

____

名字：______________________ 日期：__________

6 Answer the questions based on the illustrations.

1. 李明吃不吃薯条？Lǐ Míng chī.bù.chī shǔtiáo?

____

2. 谁喝汽水？Shéi hē qìshuǐ?

____

3. 娜娜要喝什么果汁？Nànà yào hē shén.me guǒzhī?

____

4. 小梅要喝东西吗？Xiǎoméi yào hē dōng.xī .ma?

____

7 Decide if the following statements are true or false. Correct any false ones.

1. ______ Dim sum is a big portion Chinese food that goes with tea.

____

2. ______ Teapots should be filled one half full with tea leaves.

____

3. ______ Tea-drinking habits differ depending on the age of people. Young people prefer light tastes like jasmine tea, and older people prefer strong tastes like oolong tea.

____

8 Answer the following questions in Pinyin .

1. 你喜欢喝热巧克力吗？Nǐ xǐ.huān hē rè qiǎo.kèlì .ma?

____

2. 你的兄弟姐妹喜欢喝果汁吗？他们喜欢喝什么果汁？

   Nǐ.de xiōngdì-jiěmèi xǐ.huān hē guǒzhī .ma? Tā.mén xǐ.huān hē shén.me guǒzhī?

____

3. 你通常(*usually*)点什么饮料？Nǐ tōngcháng diǎn shén.me yǐnliào?

____

Unit 4 Lesson C

1 Look at the menu and answer the questions.

价目表 jiàmùbiǎo				
馒头 mán.tóu	￥3.00	可乐 kělè	大杯 dà bēi	￥6.50
烧饼 shāobǐng	￥3.50		小杯 xiǎo bēi	￥5.50
面包 miànbāo	￥4.50	果汁 guǒzhī	大杯 dà bēi	￥6.80
煎饼 jiānbǐng	￥5.50		小杯 xiǎo bēi	￥4.80
炸鸡 zhájī	￥8.00	薯条 shǔtiáo	大 dà	￥9.00
馄饨 hún.tún	￥10.50		中 zhōng	￥7.00

1. 两个馒头多少钱？Liǎng-.ge mán.tóu duōshǎo qián?

____

2. 炸鸡、煎饼和面包，一共多少钱？Zhájī, jiānbǐng hé miàn bāo, yígòng duōshǎo qián?

____

3. 一个大杯可乐和一份中份薯条，一共多少钱？
Yì-gè dà bēi kělè hé yí-fèn zhōng fèn shǔtiáo, yígòng duōshǎo qián?

____

4. 你买一份馄饨和一个馒头，你给老板(*owner*)三十块，他要找你多少钱？
Nǐ mǎi yí-fèn hún.tún hé yí-.ge mán.tóu, *nǐ gěi lǎo*bǎn sān.shí kuài, tā yào *zhǎo* nǐ duōshǎo qián?

____

名字：__________________ 日期：__________

2 **Below are the charts showing the exchange rates between different currencies. Decide if the statements are true or false. (Note: you may need a calculator to do the exercise.)**

Euro	British pound
1	0.86

Chinese Renminbi	New Taiwanese dollar
1	4.6

Japanese Yen	Won
1	11.78

US dollar	Chinese Renminbi
1	6.8

Euro	Japanese Yen
1	148

Chinese Renminbi	Hong Kong dollar
1	1.1

_____ 1. 一块美元 yí-kuài Měiyuán ＝ 六块八毛人民币 liù-kuài bā-máo Rénmínbì

_____ 2. 一块欧元 yí-kuài Ōuyuán ＝ 七毛五分英镑 qī-máo wǔ-fēn Yīngbàng

_____ 3. 一块港币 yí-kuài Gǎngbì ＝ 一块一毛人民币 yí-kuài yī-máo Rénmínbì

_____ 4. 十五块英镑 shíwǔ-kuài Yīngbàng ＝ 二十块欧元 èr.shí-kuài Ōuyuán

_____ 5. 一百块日元 yìbǎi-kuài Rìyuán ＞ 一块欧元 yí-kuài Ōuyuán

_____ 6. 一百块人民币 yìbǎi-kuài Rénmínbì ＜ 一百块新台币 yìbǎi-kuài Xīntáibì

_____ 7. 十块新台币 shí-kuài Xīntáibì ＞ 十块港币 shí-kuài Gǎngbì

_____ 8. 一块日元 yí-kuài Rìyuán ＞ 一块韩元 yí-kuài Hányuán

_____ 9. 十块人民币 shí-kuài Rénmínbì ＜ 五块美元 wǔ-kuài Měiyuán

名字：________________ 日期：________

3 The following table shows how much money each person has. Answer the questions based on the table.

李明 Lǐ Míng	刘翔 Liú Xiáng	怡如 Yírú	小惠 Xiǎohuì

1. 谁有美元？Shéi *yǒu* Měiyuán?

____

2. 怡如有铜板吗？Yírú yǒu tóngbǎn .ma?

____

3. 谁只有钞票？Shéi *zhǐ* yǒu chāopiào?

____

4. 谁没有大钞？Shéi méiyǒu dàchāo?

____

5. 李明有多少钱？Lǐ Míng yǒu duōshǎo qián?

____

名字：____________________________ 日期：______________

4 Use 多少 *duōshǎo* to ask questions that correspond to the answers.

1. **A:** ____

   B: 我家有十三个人。Wǒ jiā yǒu shísān-.ge rén.

2. **A:** ____

   B: 这本书一百五十块钱。Zhèi-běn shū yìbǎi wǔ.shí-kuài qián.

3. **A:** ____

   B: 三明治和牛奶一共十八块钱。Sānmíngzhì hé niúnǎi yígòng shíbā-kuài qián.

4. **A:** ____

   B: 我今天喝了十四杯水。Wǒ jīn.tiān hē le shísì-bēi shuǐ.

5. **A:** ____

   B: 他们买了十五件衣服。Tā.mén mǎi le shíwǔ-jiàn yī.fú.

6. **A:** ____

   B: 我的中文课有二十二个学生。

   Wǒ.de Zhōngwén kè yǒu èr.shí’èr -.ge xué.shēng.

5 **Four people had food poisoning after they ate in the same restaurant. They don't quite remember what they ordered, so you need to figure out what they ate based on their descriptions and the menu from the restaurant. Fill in what you found out about what each of them ate.**

天天来自助餐厅 Tiān Tiān Lái Zìzhù Cāntīng

炸鸡 zhájī ￥8.75	馄饨 hùn.tún ￥12.00
可乐 kělè ￥4.25	包子 bāo.zi ￥3.00
面包 miànbāo ￥5.25	豆浆 dòujiāng ￥4.00
果汁 guǒzhī ￥6.48	馒头 mán.tóu ￥3.00
三明治 sānmíngzhì ￥5.50	牛奶 niúnǎi ￥4.50

A.

我点一杯饮料，我给老板七块，他找我五毛。*Wǒ* diǎn yī-bēi yǐnliào, *wǒ gěi lǎo*bǎn qī-kuài, tā *zhǎo wǒ* wǔ-máo.

B.

我的一共十三块，我点了吃的东西和一杯可乐。Wǒ.de yígòng shísān-kuài, *wǒ* diǎn le chī .de dōng.xī hé yì-bēi kělè.

C.

我只点一个中式早餐，十二块。
Wǒ zhǐ diǎn yí-.ge zhōngshì zǎocān, shí'èr-kuài.

D.

我买两种饮料，一共八块五毛。*Wǒ mǎi liǎng-zhǒng* yǐnliào, yígòng bā-kuài wǔ-máo.

1. A 点什么？A diǎn shén.me?

____

2. B 点什么？B diǎn shén.me?

____

3. C 点什么？C diǎn shén.me?

____

4. D 点什么？D diǎn shén.me?

____

6 Decide if the following statements are true or false. Correct any false ones.

1. _____ Chinese students usually eat sandwiches for lunch.

____

2. _____ Lunchboxes are often made by packing last night's dinner leftovers into a metallic lunchbox.

____

3. _____ School stores usually open around noon and sell simple lunchboxes or bread and milk. This is also a choice for students to buy lunches.

____

7 Answer the following questions in Pinyin .

1. 你喜欢吃什么早餐？*Nǐ* xǐ.huān chī shén.me zǎocān?

____

2. 你喜欢喝豆浆还是牛奶？*Nǐ* xǐ.huān hē dòujiāng hái.shì niúnǎi?

____

3. 你有没有人民币？*Nǐ* yǒu méi.yǒu Rénmínbì?

____

名字：______________________ 日期：__________

Unit 4 Lesson D

1 **Look at the items below and write a word that describes how each item tastes.**

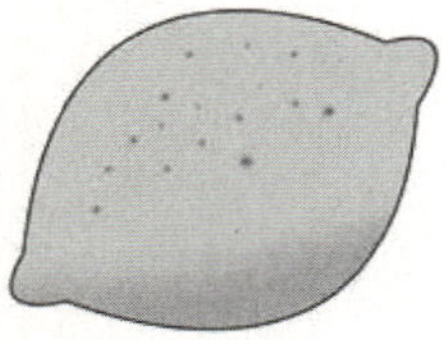

1. ____________________ 4. ____________________ 7. ____________________

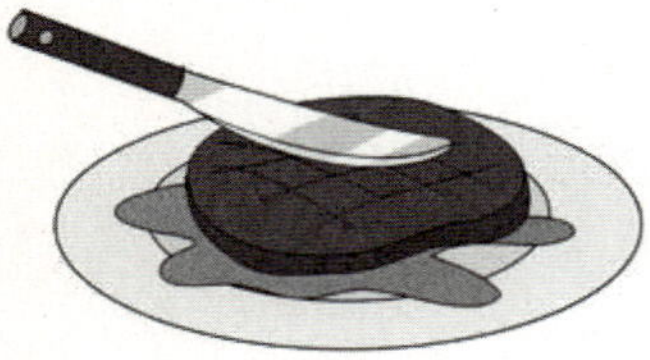

2. ____________________ 5. ____________________ 8. ____________________

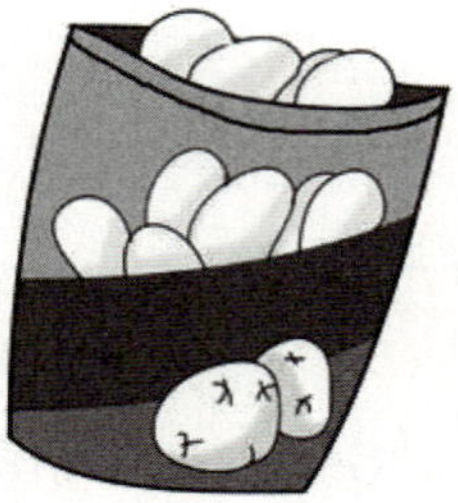

3. ____________________ 6. ____________________

名字：__________________ 日期：__________

2 Match the picture of each animal to the corresponding meat in Chinese.

1. 

2. 

3. 

4. 

5. 

A. 猪肉 zhūròu

B. 鸭肉 yāròu

C. 牛肉 niúròu

D. 羊肉 yángròu

E. 鸡肉 jīròu

3 Use the pattern *adj.* 不 *adj.* to rewrite the sentences below.

Lì.zi: 酸辣汤酸吗？ Suānlàtāng suān .ma?
酸辣汤酸不酸？ Suānlàtāng suān.bù.suān?

1. 宫保鸡丁辣吗？ Gōngbǎo jīdīng là .ma?

____

2. 牛肉面油吗？ Niúròumiàn yóu .ma?

____

3. 电子游戏好玩儿吗？ Diànzǐ yóuxì hǎowánr .ma?

____

4. 香草奶昔甜吗？ Xiāng*cǎo* nǎixí tián .ma?

____

5. 炸鸡很咸吗? Zhájī hěn xián .ma?

____

4 Fill in the blanks to complete the conversation below.

还 hái	都 dōu	份 fèn	给 gěi	要 yào
不 bù	咸 xián	马上 mǎshàng	有名 yǒumíng	

服务员：您好 Nínhǎo！请问您 Qǐngwèn nín __________点菜了吗 diǎn-cài .le .ma？

客人：饭和面我 Fàn hé miàn wǒ __________想吃 xiǎng chī，我不知道要点哪一个 wǒ bù zhī.dào yào *diǎn* nǎ yí-.ge。

服务员：我们的牛肉面很好吃 Wǒ.mén.de niúròumiàn *hěn* hǎochī，麻婆豆腐饭也很 mápó dòu.fǔ fàn *yě* hěn __________。

客人：请问牛肉面 Qǐngwèn niúròumiàn __________吗.ma？

服务员：不咸，我们的牛肉面很清淡。Bù xián, wǒ.mén.de niúròumiàn hěn qīngdàn.

客人：请问麻婆豆腐辣 Qǐngwèn mápó dòu.fǔ là __________辣 là？

服务员：麻婆豆腐很辣 Mápó dòu.*fǔ* hěn là，您喜欢吃辣的菜吗 nín xǐ.huān chī là .de cài .ma?

客人：我很喜欢吃辣的菜 *Wǒ hěn* xǐ.huān chī là .de cài，请给我一 *qǐng gěi* wǒ yí __________麻婆豆腐 mápó dòu.fǔ。

服务员：您 nín __________要什么 yào shén.me？

客人：请再 Qǐng zài __________我一碗饭 wǒ yì-wǎn fàn。

服务员：好的 hǎo .de，__________来 lái。

5 Decide if the statements are true or false. Correct any false statements.

1. _____ Rice and noodles are staple foods in China.

   ____

2. _____ Because of the weather, people in the north traditionally ate more rice and people in the south ate more noodles.

   ____

3. _____ Chinese rarely ate beef because there were not many cattle in the past. Nowadays they still don't eat much beef because they prefer chicken and pork.

   ____

6 Answer the following questions in Pinyin based on your own situation.

1. 你喜欢先(*first*)吃饭还是先(*first*)喝汤？*Nǐ* xǐ.huān xiān chī-fàn hái.shì xiān hē-tāng?

   ____

2. 你吃不吃猪肉？Nǐ chī .bù .chī zhūròu?

   ____

3. 美国菜清不清淡？Měi.guó cài qīng bù qīngdàn?

   ____

名字：________________________ 日期：____________

7 **The following article is from a gourmet magazine in Taiwan. The critic makes a comparison between two restaurants which are famous for their 鸡肉饭 *jīròufàn*. Answer the questions that are based on this article.**

香香鸡肉饭 Xiāngxiāng jīròufàn

鸡肉饭 jīròufàn：65 元 yuán
鸡蛋 jīdàn：10 元 yuán
鸡腿 jītuǐ：40 元 yuán

<u>行家评论 hángjiā pínglùn</u>

饭 fàn: ★★★★★
价钱 jià qián: ★★★
鸡肉 jīròu: ★★★★★
蛋 dàn: ★★★★

☺ 饭很好吃，鸡肉不油，蛋也很香。
Fàn *hěn* hǎochī, jīròu bù yóu, dàn *yě* hěn xiāng.

老李鸡肉饭 *Lǎo*lǐ jīròufàn

鸡肉饭 jīròufàn：45 元 yuán
鸡肉 jīròu：30 元 yuán
菜 cài：15 元 yuán

<u>行家评论 hángjiā pínglùn</u>

饭 fàn: ★★★
价钱 jià qián: ★★★★
鸡肉 jīròu: ★★★
菜 cài: ★★★

☹ 菜很油，鸡肉很清淡，很便宜，但是不好吃。
Cài hěn yóu, jīròu hěn qīngdàn, hěn pián.yí, dàn.shì bù hǎochī.

1. 哪一个鸡肉饭好吃? Nǎ yí-.ge jīròufàn hǎochī?

____

2. 这两个饭馆的鸡肉饭油不油? Zhè liǎng-.ge fànguǎn .de jīròufàn yóu .bù yóu?

____

3. 老李鸡肉饭的菜清不清淡? *Lǎo*lǐ jīròufàn .de cài qīng .bù qīngdàn?

____

4. 你在香香鸡肉饭点了一碗鸡肉饭、一个鸡蛋和两份鸡腿，一共多少钱？
Nǐ zài Xiāngxiāng jīròufàn diǎn.le yì-wǎn jīròufàn, yí-.ge jīdàn hé liǎng-fèn jītuǐ, yígòng duōshǎo qián?

____

5. 你在老李鸡肉饭点了两碗鸡肉饭、一份鸡肉和两份菜，一共多少钱？
Nǐ zài *Lǎo*lǐ jīròufàn diǎn.le *liǎng*-wǎn jīròufàn, yí-fèn jīròu hé liǎng-fèn cài, yígòng duōshǎo qián?

____

名字：________________ 日期：________

Unit 5 Lesson A

1 Fill in the blanks based on the time sequence.

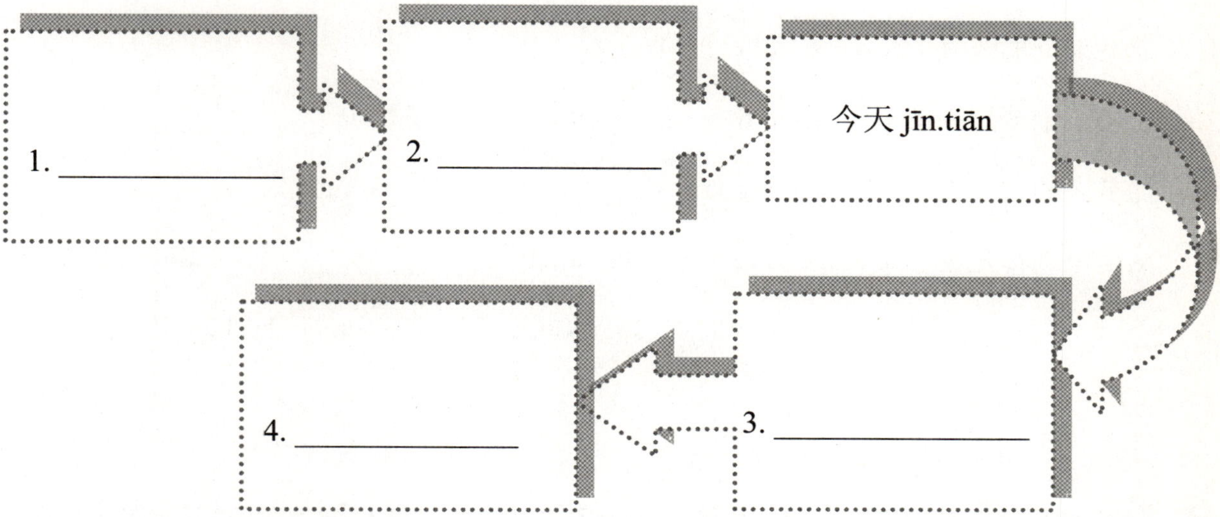

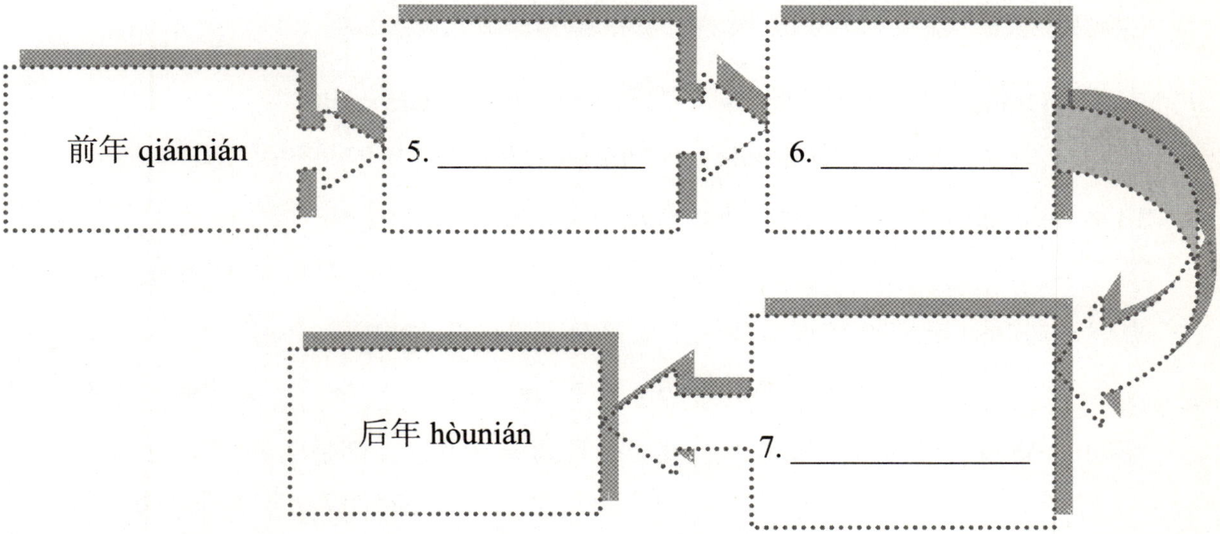

2 Complete each sentence with a word from the box.

见 jiàn	会 huì	怎么样 zěn.meyàng	真 zhēn	上 shàng

1. 北京夏天的天气 Běijīng xià.tiān .de tiān.qì_____________?
2. 明天下午五点在图书馆 Míng.tiān xià.*wǔ wǔ*-diǎn zài túshūguǎn_____________!
3. 加拿大的冬天 Jiā'nádà .de dōngtiān_____________下雪 xià-xuě。
4. 这个星期都是雨天 Zhèi.ge xīngqī dōu shì yǔ.tiān，_____________讨厌 tǎoyàn!
5. _____________个星期二是小美的生日.ge Xīngqī'èr shì *Xiǎo*měi .de shēng.rì。

3 Four students are talking about their favorite country and the weather there. Read the following descriptions and answer the questions.

书芳 Shūfāng: 我喜欢英国。英国有风，很舒服*(comfortable)*。
Wǒ xǐ.huān Yīng.guó. Yīng.guó yǒu fēng, hěn shūfú.

白苹 Bái Píng: 我喜欢台湾。台北常常下雨，我喜欢雨天。
Wǒ xǐ.huān Táiwān. Táiběi cháng.x xià-yǔ, *wǒ* xǐ.huān yǔ.tiān.

晓君 Xiǎojūn: 我喜欢德国。德国十二月会下雪，我喜欢雪。
Wǒ xǐ.huān Dé.guó. Dé.guó Shí'èryuè huì xià-xuě, *wǒ* xǐ.huān xuě.

李明 Lǐ Míng: 我喜欢西班牙。西班牙七月的天气很好，都是晴天。
Wǒ xǐ.huān Xībānyá. Xībānyá Qīyuè .de tiān.qì *hěn* hǎo, dōu shì qíng.tiān.

1. 谁喜欢雨天？Shéi xǐ.huān yǔ.tiān?

____

2. 英国的天气怎么样？Yīng.guó .de tiān.qì zěn.meyàng?

____

3. 李明喜欢阴天，对不对？Lǐ Míng xǐ.huān yīn.tiān, duì .bú .duì?

____

4 Fill in the blanks based on what you learned in the Culture Window.

1. Beihai Park is the oldest surviving ______________ garden to be built in the world.

2. Beihai Park is famous for its "one ______________, three ______________."

3. The suns, moons, and flames decorated on Yong'an Temple represent the brightness of the light of ______________.

名字：____________________ 日期：____________

5 Answer the following questions in Pinyin according to your own situation.

1. 你喜欢雨天还是晴天？*Nǐ* xǐ.huān yǔ.tiān hái.shì qíng.tiān?

____

2. 今天天气冷不冷？Jīn.tiān tiān.qì lěng .bù lěng?

____

3. 上个周末你做了什么？Shàng.ge zhōumò nǐ zuò .le shén.me?

____

4. 你的国家十二月天气怎么样？Nǐ .de guójiā Shí’èryuè tiān.qì zěn.meyàng?

____

6 **The chart below is the weather forecast for February. Fill in the blanks in the first week with the type of weather that matches the picture and then answer the questions.**

星期日 Xīngqīrì	星期一 Xīngqīyī	星期二 Xīngqī'èr	星期三 Xīngqīsān	星期四 Xīngqīsì	星期五 Xīngqīwǔ	星期六 Xīngqīliù
1  ________	2  ________	3  ________	4  ________	5  ________	6  ________	7  ________
8 	9 	10 	11 	12. 	13 	14 
15 	16 	17 	18 	19 	20 	21 
22 	23 	24 	25 	26 	27 	28 

1. 今天天气怎么样？Jīn.tiān tiān.qì zěn.meyàng?

____

2. 昨天天气怎么样？Zuó.tiān tiān.qì zěn.meyàng?

____

3. 这个星期天气怎么样？Zhèi.ge xīng.qī tiānqì zěn.meyàng?

____

4. 这个月 28 号天气怎么样？Zhèi.ge yuè èr.shíbā hào tiān.qì zěn.meyàng?

____

5. 下下个星期四天气怎么样？Xià.x-.ge Xīngqīsì tiān.qì zěn.meyàng?

____

6. 李明想在这个月的周末跟朋友去海边，哪天去好？
Lǐ Míng xiǎng zài zhèi.ge yuè .de zhōumò gēn péng.yǒu qù hǎibiān, něi-tiān qù hǎo?

____

名字：______________________ 日期：__________

7 **Poets are influenced by their environment. Look at the following poems and match each one to the weather that influenced the poet.**

1. 清明时节雨纷纷，路上行人欲断魂。Qīngmíng shíjié yǔ fēn.x, lù shàng xíngrén yù duànhún.

2. 天苍苍，野茫茫，风吹草低见牛羊。Tiān cāng.x, yě máng.x, fēng chuī cǎo dī xiàn niú yáng.

3. 梅子黄时日日晴，小溪泛尽却山行。Méi.zi huáng shí rì.x qíng, xiǎo xī fàn jìn què shān xíng.

A. 刮风 guā-fēng　　B. 晴天 qíng.tiān　　C. 雨天 yǔ.tiān

名字：________________________ 日期：____________

Unit 5 Lesson B

1 **Match each picture to its corresponding season and weather condition.**

春天 chūn.tiān ◆

◆ 热 rè

夏天 xià.tiān ◆

◆ 凉 liáng

秋天 qiū.tiān ◆

◆ 温暖 wēnnuǎn

冬天 dōng.tiān ◆

◆ 冷 lěng

2 Look at the thermometers, and write the temperature with the correct unit of measurement (Celsius or Fahrenheit).

Lì.zi: 摄氏二十三度。Shèshì èrshí sān dù.

1.

____

3.

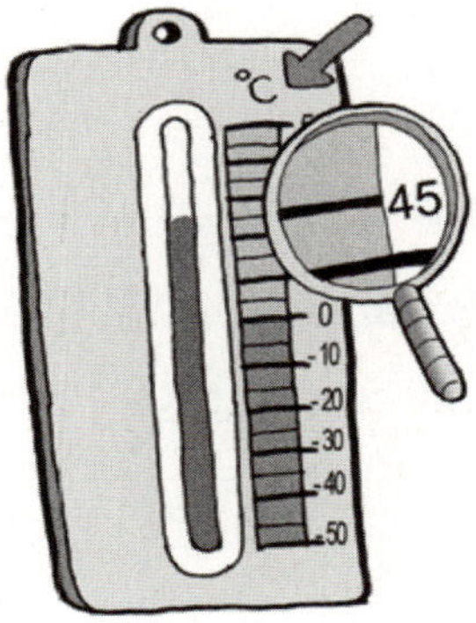

____

5.

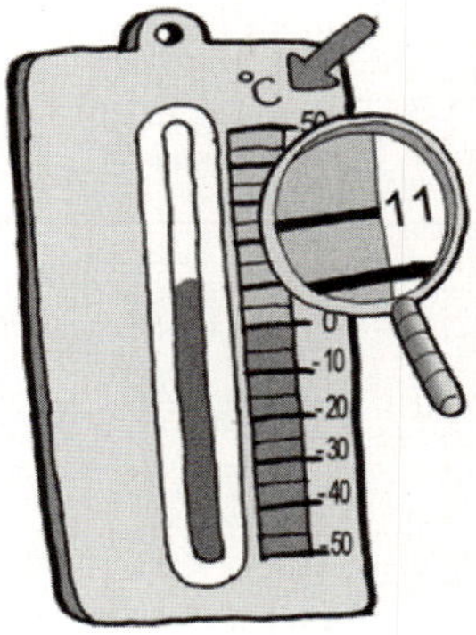

____

2.

____

4.

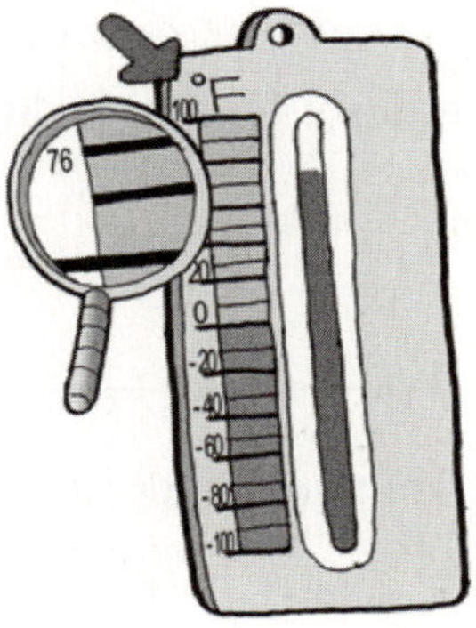

____

6.

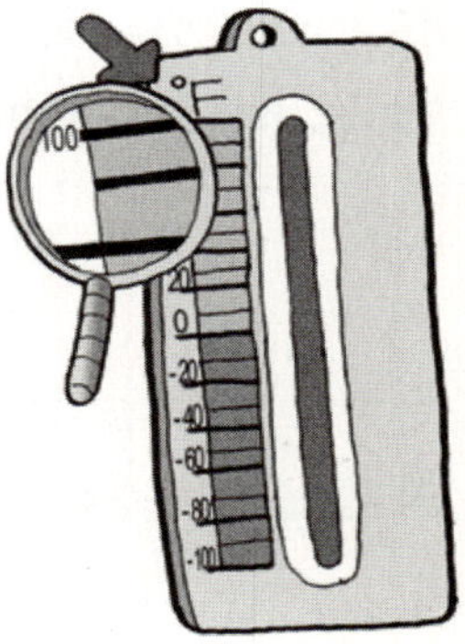

____

3 Answer the questions using the two charts below.

The Four Seasons in Hainan	
三月 ~ 五月	18°C ~ 26°C
六月 ~ 八月	28°C~ 37°C
九月 ~ 十一月	20°C~ 25°C
十二月 ~ 二月	15°C~ 18°C

Celsius (°C)	Fahrenheit (°F)
10°C	50°F
20°C	68°F
30°C	86°F
40°C	104°F
F = C × 9/5 + 32	

1. 夏天的时候，天气很热吗？Xià.tiān .de shí.hòu, tiān.qì hěn rè .ma?

____

2. 秋天的时候，最高温度(*the highest temperature*)是摄氏几度？
   Qiū.tiān .de shí.hòu, zuì gāo wēndù shì Shèshì jǐ-dù?

____

3. 冬天的时候，要暖气吗？Dōng.tiān .de shí.hòu, yào nuǎnqì .ma?

____

4. 春天的时候，最低温度(*the lowest temperature*)是华氏几度？
   Chūn.tiān .de shí.hòu, zuì dī wēndù shì Huáshì jǐ-dù?

____

5. 海南岛的四季，天气怎么样？Hǎinándǎo .de sì-jì, tiān.qì zěn.meyàng?

____

名字：______________________ 日期：__________

4 Decide if each statement is true or false based on the information provided.

冰淇淋口味 bīngqílín kǒuwèi	巧克力 qiǎo.kèlì	香草 xiāngcǎo	草莓 cǎoméi	抹茶 mǒchá
小芳 Xiǎofāng	♥	♥		
强强 Qiángqiáng	♥			
美莉 Měilì	♥		♥	
小派 Xiǎopài				♥
文森 Wénsēn		♥	♥	

1. ______ 有两个人喜欢香草口味的冰淇淋。

   Yǒu liǎng-.ge rén xǐ.huān xiāngcǎo kǒuwèi .de bīng.qílín.

2. ______ 文森喜欢香草和草莓口味的冰淇淋。

   Wénsēn xǐ.huān xiāngcǎo hé cǎoméi kǒuwèi .de bīng.qílín.

3. ______ 没有人喜欢抹茶口味的冰淇淋。

   Méiyǒu rén xǐ.huān mǒchá kǒuwèi .de bīng.qílín.

4. ______ 小派觉得抹茶口味的冰淇淋比较好吃。

   Xiǎopài jué.de mǒchá kǒuwèi .de bīng.qílín bǐjiào hǎochī.

5. ______ 小芳只喜欢吃巧克力口味的冰淇淋。

   Xiǎofāng zhǐ xǐ.huān chī qiǎo.kèlì kǒuwèi .de bīng.qílín.

6. ______ 有三个人喜欢巧克力口味的冰淇淋。

   Yǒu sān-.ge rén xǐ.huān qiǎo.kèlì kǒuwèi .de bīng.qílín.

7. ______ 美莉觉得巧克力和草莓口味的冰淇淋比较好吃。

   Měilì jué.de qiǎo.kèlì hé cǎoméi kǒuwèi .de bīng.qílín bǐjiào hǎochī.

8. ______ 强强喜欢芝麻和香草口味的冰淇淋。

   Qiángqiáng xǐ.huān zhī.má hé xiāngcǎo kǒuwèi .de bīng.qílín.

5 Use the pattern 又……又……*yòu… yòu…* to write complete sentences.

Lì.zi: 我 wǒ / 饿 è / 渴 kě
我又饿又渴。Wǒ yòu è yòu kě.

1. 饮料 yǐnliào / 冰 bīng / 好喝 hǎohē

____

2. 今天的天气 jīn.tiān .de tiān.qì / 刮风 guā-fēng / 下雨 xià-yǔ

____

3. 他 tā / 学 xué / 中文 Zhōngwén / 日文 Rìwén

____

4. 酸辣汤 suānlàtāng / 酸 suān / 辣 là

____

5. 草莓 cǎoméi / 甜 tián / 好吃 hǎochī

____

6. 弟弟 dì.x / 吃 chī / 热狗 règǒu / 薯条 shǔtiáo

____

名字：____________________________ 日期：_____________

6 **You are now working in a high-class ice cream shop. Your job is to collect information from the surveys below about how the four Ice Cream Experts (ICE) feel about each ice cream flavor. Use the pattern 太……了 *tài …….le* to fill out your report.**

ICE 1

Chocolate: too sweet
Strawberry: too sour
Red bean: too sweet
Matcha: very good

ICE 2

Chocolate: very good
Strawberry: too sour
Red bean: too sweet
Matcha: bitter

ICE 3

Chocolate: yummy
Strawberry: not bad
Red bean: too sweet
Matcha: too bitter

ICE 4

Chocolate: not bad
Strawberry: too sour
Red bean: too sweet
Matcha: too bitter

Q: 巧克力口味怎么样？Qiǎo.kèlì kǒuwèi zěn.meyàng?

A: ICE 1 觉得 jué.de________________。

Q: 草莓口味怎么样？Cǎoméi kǒuwèi zěn.meyàng?

A: ICE 1、ICE 2、ICE 4 觉得 jué.de ________________。

Q: 红豆口味怎么样？Hóngdòu kǒuwèi zěn.meyàng?

A: 他们都觉得 Tā.mén dōu jué.de________________。

Q: 抹茶口味怎么样？Mǒchá kǒuwèi zěn.meyàng?

A: ICE 2、ICE 3、ICE 4 觉得 jué.de ________________。

7 Fill in the blanks based on what you learned in the Culture Window.

1. Emperor Qin Shi Huang first standardized units of measure in China in ______________ Dynasty (221-207 B.C.).

2. The six important sports in China refer to __________, __________, soccer, __________, __________, and tennis.

3. There are not many countries in the world that can compete with China in __________ and __________.

8 Answer the following questions in Pinyin according to your own situation.

1. 夏天睡觉的时候，你开空调吗? Xià.tiān shuì-jiào .de shí.hòu, nǐ kāi kōngtiáo .ma?

____

2. 冬天的时候，你开不开暖气？Dōng.tiān .de shí.hòu, nǐ kāi .bù kāi nuǎnqì?

____

3. 你喜欢吃什么口味的冰淇淋？*Nǐ* xǐ.huān chī shén.me kǒuwèi .de bīng.qílín?

____

4. 你渴的时候，喝水还是饮料？*Nǐ* kě .de shí.hòu, hē shuǐ hái.shì yǐnliào?

____

名字：______________________ 日期：__________

Unit 5 Lesson C

1 Draw a line from each picture to its corresponding festival and date.

春节 ◆
Chūnjié

◆ 一月一号
Yīyuè yī hào

清明 ◆
Qīngmíng

◆ 三月三号
Sānyuè sān hào

中秋节 ◆
Zhōngqiūjié

◆ 五月五号
Wǔyuè wǔ hào

端午节 ◆
Duānwǔjié

◆ 八月十五号
Bāyuè shíwǔ hào

2 Look at the chart below and answer the questions.

Chinese Holiday/Festival	Chinese Lunar Date
New Year's Eve	December 31st
Chinese New Year	January 1st
Lantern Festival	January 15th
Tomb-sweeping Festival	March 3rd
Dragon Boat Festival	May 5th
Mid-Autumn Festival	August 15th
Double Ninth Festival	September 9th

1. 中秋节是哪天？Zhōngqiūjié shì něi-tiān?

____

2. 元宵节是在一月初吗？Yuánxiāojié shì zài Yīyuè chū .ma?

____

3. 清明节在三月中吗？Qīngmíngjié zài Sānyuè zhōng .ma?

____

4. 现在是八月初，什么节快到了？Xiànzài shì Bāyuè chū, shén.me jié kuài dào .le?

____

5. 昨天是五月四号，今天是什么节？
Zuó.tiān shì Wǔyuè sì hào, jīn.tiān shì shén.me jié?

____

3 Match each sentence to its correct response.

A. 今天是十二月二十号。Jīn.tiān shì Shí'éryuè èr.shí hào.

B. 真讨厌！暑假快结束了。Zhēn tǎoyàn! Shǔjià kuài jiéshù .le.

C. 你几月几号回美国？*Nǐ* jǐ-yuè jǐ-hào huí Měi.guó?

D. 为什么你喜欢中国新年？Wèishén.me *nǐ* xǐ.huān Zhōng.guó Xīnnián?

E. 这家餐厅有宫保鸡丁吗？Zhèi-jiā cāntīng yǒu gōngbǎo jīdīng .ma?

F. 中国新年是哪一天？Zhōng.guó Xīnnián shì nǎ-yì tiān?

G. 你为什么点这么多东西？Nǐ wèishén.me diǎn zhè.me duō dōng.xī?

1. ______ 因为我又饿又渴。Yīnwèi wǒ yòu è yòu kě.

2. ______ 五月初。Wǔyuè chū.

3. ______ 因为可以拿红包、放鞭炮。Yīnwèi *kě*yǐ ná-hóngbāo, fang-biānpào.

4. ______ 圣诞节快到了！Shèngdànjié kuài dào .le!

5. ______ 我不觉得讨厌，我喜欢新学期。Wǒ bù jué.de tǎoyàn, *wǒ* xǐ.huān xīn xuéqī.

6. ______ 得看菜单上有没有。Děi kàn càidān shàng yǒu méi.yǒu.

7. ______ 中国新年通常在一月底到二月初。

   Zhōng.guó Xīnnián tōngcháng zài Yīyuè dǐ dào Èryuè chū.

4 Use the pattern 因为…所以…*yīnwèi…suǒyǐ…* to answer the following questions.

Li.zi: 为什么你点冰淇淋？
Wèishén.me *nǐ* diǎn bīngqílín?
因为今天很热，所以我想吃冰的东西。
Yīnwèi jīn.tiān hěn rè, *suǒ*yǐ *wǒ* xiǎng chī bīng .de dōng.xī.

1. 为什么他不喜欢吃宫保鸡丁？Wèishén.me tā bù xǐ.huān chī gōngbǎo jīdīng?

   ____

2. 为什么你这个周末要去图书馆？Wèishén.me nǐ zhèi-.ge zhōumò yào qù túshūguǎn?

   ____

3. 为什么你学中文？Wèishén.me nǐ xué Zhōngwén?

   ____

4. 为什么你喜欢中国新年？Wèishén.me *nǐ* xǐ.huān Zhōng.guó Xīnnián?

   ____

名字：______________________ 日期：__________

5 Fill in the blanks based on what you learned from the Culture Window.

1. Chinese Lunar New Year is also known as ____________, which is a very important traditional festival that the Chinese celebrate on the ____________ day of the first month of the ____________ calendar.
2. On New Year's Eve, the dinner usually includes dishes that are "____________", such as ____________ (a homonym for 'surplus') and dumplings (to represent riches).
3. There are ____________ animals in Chinese Zodiac.

6 Answer the following questions in Pinyin according to your own situation.

1. 在你的国家你们怎么过年？Zài nǐ.de guójiā nǐ.mén zěn.me guònián?

   ____

2. 你觉得中国新年有意思吗？Nǐ jué.de Zhōngguó Xīnnián yǒu yì.sī .ma?

   ____

3. 你们家用(*to use*)农历吗？Nǐ.mén jiā yòng nónglì .ma?

   ____

名字：____________________ 日期：__________

7 Use 快要 *kuài yào* or 已经 *yǐjīng* to describe the pictures.

1. 他 Tā ____________________ 到学校了 dào xuéxiào .le。

2. 他们 Tā.mén ____________________ 吃饱了 chī bǎo .le。

3. 电影 Diànyǐng ____________________ 结束(*to finish*)了 jiéshù .le。

4. 考试 Kǎoshì ____________________ 到了 dào .le。

名字：________________ 日期：________

8 Read Xiaoqiang's diary entry and answer the questions that follow.

五月五日 Wǔyuè wǔ rì　　星期五 Xīngqīwǔ

天气晴 tiān.qì qíng

因为今天是端午节，所以我不用去学校。我跟朋友去篮球场打篮球。天气好热，真讨厌！大概(*probably*)是摄氏三十五度吧！我又热又渴，所以我去冰淇淋店点了一个草莓冰淇淋。我也想喝东西，所以我到饮料店点了一杯大杯可乐。喝东西以后，我觉得很饿，所以我去快餐店买了一个大汉堡包和一份大的薯条。我现在很累，我想去睡觉了。Yīnwèi jīn.tiān shì Duānwǔjié, *suǒyǐ* wǒ búyòng qù xuéxiào. Wǒ gēn péng.yǒu qù lánqiúchǎng dǎ-lánqiú. Tiān.qì hǎo rè, zhēn tǎoyàn! Dàgài shì Shèshì sān.shíwǔ-dù .ba! Wǒ yòu rè yòu kě, *suǒyǐ* wǒ qù bīng.qílín diàn diǎn .le yí-.ge cǎoméi bīng.qílín. *Wǒ yě* xiǎng hē dōng.xī, *suǒyǐ* wǒ dào yǐnliào diàn diǎn .le yì-bēi dà bēi kělè. Hē dōng.xī yǐhòu, wǒ jué.de hěn è, *suǒyǐ* wǒ qù kuàicāndiàn mǎi .le yí-.ge dà hànbǎobāo hé yí-fèn dà .de shǔtiáo. Wǒ xiànzài hěn lèi, *wǒ* xiǎng qù shuìjiào .le.

1. 为什么小强今天不去学校？Wèishén.me Xiǎoqiáng jīn.tiān bú qù xuéxiào?

____

2. 小强今天去哪里？Xiǎoqiáng jīn.tiān qù *nǎlǐ*?

____

3. 今天天气怎么样？Jīn.tiān tiān.qì zěn.meyàng?

____

4. 今天几度？Jīn.tiān jǐ-dù?

____

5. 小强点了什么口味的冰淇淋？Xiǎoqiáng diǎn .le shén.me kǒuwèi .de bīng.qílín?

____

6. 小强点了什么喝的东西？Xiǎoqiáng diǎn .le shén.me hē .de dōng.xī?

____

7. 小强吃了什么？Xiǎoqiáng chī .le shén.me?

____

8. 小强去哪里买了吃的东西？Xiǎoqiáng qù *nǎlǐ* mǎi .le chī .de dōng.xī?

____

9. 小强现在想做什么？Xiǎoqiáng xiànzài xiǎng zuò shén.me?

____

Unit 5 Lesson D

1 Draw a line from each picture to its corresponding festival and date.

端午节 ◆
Duānwǔjié

◆ 七月七号
Qīyuè qī hào

七夕 ◆
Qīxī

◆ 七月十五号
Qīyuè shíwǔ hào

中元节 ◆
Zhōngyuánjié

◆ 五月五号
Wǔyuè wǔ hào

冬至 ◆
Dōngzhì

◆ 十二月二十二号
Shí’èryuè èr.shí’èr hào

2 **Write the name of the Chinese festival based on how each pea describes his or her day.**

1.

因为我今天帮妈妈包粽子，所以她买新的香包送给我，我很高兴！Yīnwèi wǒ jīn.tiān bāng mā.x bāo zòng.zi, *suǒ*yǐ tā mǎi xīn .de xiāngbāo sòng *gěi* wǒ, *wǒ* hěn gāoxìng!

____

2.

今天天气真冷！晚上跟家人一起吃汤圆，真好！Jīn.tiān tiān.qì zhēn lěng! Wǎn.shàng gēn jiārén yìqǐ chī tāngyuán, zhēn hǎo!

____

3.

我今天晚上跟男朋友一起去法国餐厅吃饭，他送我巧克力和花！Wǒ jīn.tiān wǎn.shàng gēn nán péng.yǒu yìqǐ qù Fǎ.guó cāntīng chī-fàn, tā sòng *wǒ* qiǎokèlì hé huā!

____

名字：______________________ 日期：__________

3 Each of the following sentences has one incorrect Chinese character. Circle the wrong Chinese character and write the correct replacement on the line.

1. ______ 因为明天是端午节，所以妈妈现再包粽子。

   Yīnwèi míng.tiān shì Duānwǔjié, *suǒ*yǐ mā.x xiànzài zài bāo zòng.zi.

2. ______ 端午节除了吃粽子以外，我们也划龙周。

   Duānwǔjié chú.le chī zòng.zi yǐwài, wǒ.mén yě huá lóngzhōu.

3. ______ 为了篮球匕赛，哥哥每天都练习(*to practice*)。

   Wèi.le lánqiú bǐsài, gē.x měitiān dōu liànxí.

4. ______ 爸爸这个周末要代我们去划船。

   Bà.x zhèi-.ge zhōumò yào dài wǒ. mén qù huá-chuán.

5. ______ 因为可以拿红包，所以大加都喜欢中国新年。

   Yīnwèi *kě*yǐ ná hóngbāo, *suǒ*yǐ dàjiā dōu xǐ.huān Zhōng.guó Xīnnián.

6. ______ 除了包粽子以外，中国人也做箱包。

   Chú.le bāo zòng.zi yǐwài, Zhōng.guórén yě zuò xiāngbāo.

7. ______ 东至的时候，大家会吃汤圆。

   Dōngzhì .de shíhòu, dàjiā huì chī tāngyuán.

8. ______ 划船一点儿也不男！ Huá-chuán yì.diǎnr yě bù nán.

名字：________________________ 日期：____________

4 **Sabrina's just returned from a trip to China. Read her blog posting below and answer the following questions.**

一月，是新的一年，我今年除了学中文以外，还要学日文，加油！
Yīyuè, shì xīn .de yì nián, wǒ jīnnián chú.le xué Zhōngwén yǐwài, hái yào xué Rìwén, jiāyóu!

二月，因为我加入书法社，所以我认识了很多新朋友。
Èryuè, yīnwèi wǒ jiārù shūfǎshè, *suǒyǐ* wǒ rènshì .le hěn duō xīn péng.yǒu.

三月，春天到了，每天都是晴天！ Sānyuè, chūn.tiān dào.le, měitiān dōu shì qíngtiān.

四月，这个月我有七天的假期，所以我回美国去看家人。
Sìyuè, zhèi-.ge yuè *wǒ* yǒu qī-tiān .de jiàqí, *suǒyǐ* wǒ huí Měi.guó qù kàn jiārén.

五月，端午节我吃了十个粽子，还看龙舟比赛，真有意思！
Wǔyuè, Duānwǔjié wǒ chī.le shí-.ge zòng.zi, hái kàn lóngzhōu bǐsài, zhēn yǒu yì.sī.

六月，学期结束！ Liùyuè, xuéqī jiéshù!

七月，天气好热，听说七月七是七夕。Qīyuè, tiān.qì hǎo rè, tīngshuō Qīyuè qī shì Qīxī.

八月，我的中国朋友带我去爬山，好累啊！
Bāyuè, wǒ.de Zhōng.guó péng.yǒu dài wǒ qù páshān, hǎo lèi .ā!

九月，学期开始了，很开心见到好久不见的同学们。中秋节那天，我吃月饼，还赏月。
Jiǔyuè, xuéqī kāishǐ .le, hěn kāixīn jiàndào *hǎo* jiǔ bú jiàn .de tóngxué.mén. Zhōngqiūjié nèi-tiān, wǒ chī yuèbǐng, hái shǎngyuè.

十月，天气变冷了。Shíyuè, tiān.qì biàn lěng .le.

十一月，我每天都读中文。Shíyīyuè, *wǒ* měitiān dōu dú Zhōngwén.

十二月，冬至那一天吃汤圆。十二月底，我和朋友去巴黎(*Paris*)过除夕(*Chinese New Year's Eve*)。Shí'èryuè, Dōngzhì nà yì-tiān chī tāngyuán. Shí'èryuè dǐ, Wǒ hé péng.yǒu qù Bālí guò Chúxī.

名字：________________________ 日期：__________

1. Sabrina 学什么语言(*language*)？ Sabrina xué shén.me yǔyán?
(use the pattern 除了……以外，也 / 还…… *chú.le……yǐwài, yě / hái* to answer)

____

2. 中国春天的天气怎么样？ Zhōng.guó chūn.tiān .de tiān.qì zěn.meyàng?

____

3. 端午节 Sabrina 做什么？ Duānwǔjié Sabrina zuò shén.me?

____

4. 七月的天气还很凉吗？ Qīyuè .de tiān.qì hái hěn liáng .ma?
(use 一点儿也 / 都不 *yì.diǎnr yě / dōu bù* to answer this question)

____

5. Sabrina 中秋节那天做什么？ Sabrina Zhōngqiūjié nèi-tiān zuò shén.me?

____

6. Sabrina 几月回美国？ 她为什么回美国？
Sabrina jǐ-yuè huí Měi.guó? Tā wèishén.me huí Měi.guó?

____

5 Match each sentence with its correct response.

A. 昨天晚上十一点，你还在上网吗？

Zuó.tiān wǎn.shàng shíyī-diǎn, nǐ hái zài shàngwǎng .ma?

B. 妈妈做什么晚餐？Mā.x zuò shén.me wǎncān?

C. 你的同学都是美国人吧？

Nǐ.de tóngxué dōu shì Měi.guórén .ba?

D. 他喜欢吃粽子吗？Tā xǐ.huān chī zòng.zi .ma?

E. 中文课很难吧？Zhōngwén kè hěn nán .ba?

F. 今天下午李明只打篮球吗？

Jīn.tiān xià.wǔ Lǐ Míng *zhǐ* dǎ-lánqiú .ma?

1. ________ 除了意大利面，还有色拉。Chú.le Yìdàlìmiàn, hái yǒu sèlā.

2. ________ 他一点儿都不喜欢。Tā yì.diǎnr dōu bù xǐ.huān.

3. ________ 我已经睡觉了。*Wǒ* yǐjīng shuì-jiào .le.

4. ________ 除了篮球以外，他还去游泳。Chú.le lánqiú yǐwài, tā hái qù yóuyǒng.

5. ________ 一点儿也不难。我觉得中文课很好玩儿！
Yì.diǎnr yě bù nán. Wǒ jué.de Zhōngwén kè *hěn* hǎowánr!

6. ________ 除了李明以外，我的同学都是美国人。

Chú.le Lǐ Míng yǐwài, wǒ.de tóngxué dōu shì Měi.guórén.

6 Fill in the blanks based on what you learned from the Culture Window.

1. The three major Chinese festivals are __________________,

   __________________, and __________________.

2. Zongzi are made of sticky rice and other ingredients that are wrapped in

   ____________ leaves. Some zongzi are ____________, and some are salty.

3. The Chinese placed antibacterial herbs into cloth sachets and wore them around their

   necks to ward off ____________ and ____________ because of health reasons.

7 Answer the following questions in Pinyin according to your own situation.

1. 你喜欢吃粽子吗？ Nǐ xǐ.huān chī zòng.zi .ma?

   ____

2. 除了中文以外，你还学什么语言(*language*)？
   Chú.le Zhōngwén yǐwài, nǐ hái xué shén.me yǔyán?

   ____

3. 今天早上八点，你在吃早餐吗？ Jīn.tiān zǎo.shàng bā-diǎn, nǐ zài chī zǎocān .ma?

   ____

Unit 6 Lesson A

1 **You are a judge at a fashion show. Match each model to her final score card.**

1. 吊带衫 diàodàishān
★★★

2. 西装 xīzhuāng
★★

3. 连衣裙 liányīqún
★★★★★

4. 衬衫 chènshān + 裙子 qún.zi
★★★★

5. 大衣 dàyī + 毛衣 máoyī + 裙子 qún.zi
★★★★★

A.

B.

C.

D.

E.

名字：________________ 日期：________

2 Draw a map in the blank space according to the descriptions below.

Side A

书店在手机店右边。Shūdiàn zài shǒujīdiàn yòu.biān.

百货商店在书店右边。Bǎihuò shāngdiàn zài shūdiàn yòu.biān.

宠物店在手机店左边。Chǒngwùdiàn zài shǒujīdiàn zuǒ.biān.

Side B

中国餐厅在快餐店右边。Zhōng.guó cāntīng zài kuàicāndiàn yòu.biān.

饮料店在冰淇淋店右边。Yǐnliàodiàn zài bīngqílíndiàn yòu.biān.

饮料店在快餐店左边。Yǐnliàodiàn zài kuàicāndiàn zuǒ.biān.

Side A

马路 mǎlù *road*

Side B

名字：________________ 日期：________

3 Use 自己 *zìjǐ* to rewrite the following sentences.

1. 小英做晚餐。Xiǎoyīng zuò wǎncān.

____

2. 我今天下课以后要去百货商店。Wǒ jīn.tiān xià-kè yǐhòu yào qù bǎihuò shāngdiàn.

____

3. 林小姐喜欢旅行。Lín *xiǎo*jiě xǐ.huān lǚxíng.

____

4. 哥哥这个周末要去海边。Gē.x zhèi-.ge zhōumò yào qù hǎibiān.

____

5. 国华下午三点以前得去图书馆。Guóhuá xià.wǔ sān-diǎn yǐqián děi qù túshūguǎn.

____

6. 李明今年要回墨西哥。Lǐ Míng jīnnián yào huí Mòxīgē.

____

4 Match each sentence to its correct response.

A. 下课以后你要去哪里？Xiàkè yǐhòu nǐ yào qù *nǎ*.lǐ?

B. 这个周末要不要跟我一起去海边游泳？

Zhèi-.ge zhōumò yào bú yào gēn wǒ yìqǐ qù hǎibiān yóuyǒng?

C. 她今天穿什么衣服？Tā jīn.tiān chuān shén.me yī.fú?

D. 你今年暑假要和朋友一起去中国旅行吗？

Nǐ jīnnián shǔjià yào hé péng.yǒu yìqǐ qù Zhōng.guó lǚxíng .ma?

E. 为什么哥哥要去宠物店？Wèishén.me gē.x yào qù chǒngwùdiàn?

F. 妈妈要买几条裤子？Mā.x yào *mǎi* jǐ-tiáo kù.zi?

G. 你七月以前去中国吗？Nǐ Qīyuè yǐqián qù Zhōng.guó .ma?

1. _______ 不好意思，这个周末我得跟我姐姐去百货商店。

Bù hǎoyì.sī, zhèi-.ge zhōumò *wǒ* děi gēn *wǒ* jiě.x qù bǎihuò shāngdiàn.

2. _______ 她今天穿背心和裙子。Tā jīn.tiān chuān bèixīn hé qún.zi.

3. _______ 不，我要自己去。Bù, wǒ yào zìjǐ qù.

4. _______ 三条，一条给她自己，两条给爸爸。

Sān-tiáo, yì-tiáo gěi tā zìjǐ, liǎng-tiáo gěi bà.x.

5. _______ 因为他想买一只小狗。Yīnwèi tā *xiǎng* mǎi yì-zhī *xiǎo*gǒu

6. _______ 我要去小明家玩电子游戏。Wǒ yào qù Xiǎomíng jiā wán diànzǐ yóuxì.

7. _______ 不，我七月以后去，七月以前去日本。

Bù, wǒ Qīyuè yǐhòu qù, Qīyuè yǐqián qù Rìběn.

5 Choose the best answer.

1. _____ Which of the following statements is true about the relationships between China and Japan?

   A. China has been influenced by Japan for a very long time.
   B. China's first interaction with Japan was before the turn of the century.
   C. The interaction between China and Japan reached a peak from the 7th century to the 10th century.

2. _____ Which is not a shared characteristic between Japanese kimonos and Chinese-style clothing?

   A. long skirts B. wide sleeves C. overlapping lapels

3. _____ Which of the following is not included in the "three daos"?

   A. chadou (dao of tea) B. kado (dao of flowers) C. shodo (dao of books)

6 Write the kind of store each of these people should go to based on the items that they are thinking about.

1. ______________________

2. ______________________

名字：________________ 日期：__________

3. ____________________

4. ____________________

7 Read the statements and answer the questions.

1. 今年是一九九八年，妈妈五十年以前出生 (*to be born*)。
Jīnnián shì yī *jiǔ* jiǔ bā nián, mā.x wǔ.shí nián yǐqián chūshēng.

Q: 妈妈的生日是哪一年？Mā.x .de shēng.rì shì nǎ-yì nián?

____

2. 今年是二零零零年，哥哥一九九六年去美国念书。
Jīnnián shì èr líng líng líng nián, gē.x yī *jiǔ* jiǔ liù nián qù Měi.guó niàn-shū.

Q: 哥哥几年以前去的美国？Gē.x jǐ-nián yǐqián qù .de Měi.guó?

____

3. 去法国旅行要三千块，姐姐一年可以存(*to save*)一千五百块。

Qù Fǎ.guó lǚxíng yào sān-qiān kuài, jiě.x yì-nián *kě*yǐ cún yìqiān *wǔ*-bǎi kuài.

Q: 姐姐几年以后可以去法国旅行？Jiě.x jǐ-nián yǐhòu *kě*yǐ qù Fǎ.guó lǚxíng?

____

4. 今天是六月一日，九月一日新学期开始(*to start*)。

Jīn.tiān shì Liùyuè yī rì, Jiǔyuè yī rì xīn xuéqī kāishǐ.

Q: 新学期几个月以后开始？Xīn xuéqī jǐ-.ge yuè yǐhòu kāishǐ?

____

5. 小明每天下午四点下课，现在是上午十点。

Xiǎomíng měitiān xià.wǔ sì-diǎn xià-kè, xiànzài shì shàng.wǔ shí-diǎn.

Q: 小明几个小时以后可以下课？Xiǎomíng jǐ-.ge xiǎoshí yǐhòu *kě*yǐ xià-kè?

____

6. 小英星期一有化学考试，星期二有历史小考，星期四有英文、数学大考。

Xiǎoyīng Xīngqīyī yǒu huàxué kǎoshì, Xīngqī'èr yǒu lìshǐ *xiǎo*kǎo, Xīngqī'sì yǒu Yīngwén, shùxué dàkǎo.

Q: 小英星期五以前有几个考试？Xiǎoyīng Xīngqī*wǔ* yǐqián *yǒu* jǐ-.ge kǎoshì?

____

名字：________________ 日期：________

8 Answer the following questions.

1. 天气很热的时候你穿什么？Tiān.qì hěn rè .de shíhòu nǐ chuān shén.me?

____

2. 天气冷的时候你穿什么？Tiān.qì lěng .de shíhòu nǐ chuān shén.me?

____

3. 你什么时候(*when*)穿连衣裙 / 西装？
Nǐ shén.me shíhòu chuān liányīqún / xīzhuāng?

____

4. 你有几件外套？
Nǐ yǒu jǐ-jiàn wàitào?

____

5. 你喜欢穿衬衫吗？
Nǐ xǐ.huān chuān chènshān .ma?

____

6. 你想自己去旅行吗？
Nǐ xiǎng zìjǐ qù lǚxíng .ma?

____

名字：______________________ 日期：__________

Unit 6 Lesson B

1 Write the most common color of each item.

Lì.zi:

红色 hóng.sè

1. ____________________ 3. ____________________ 5. ____________________

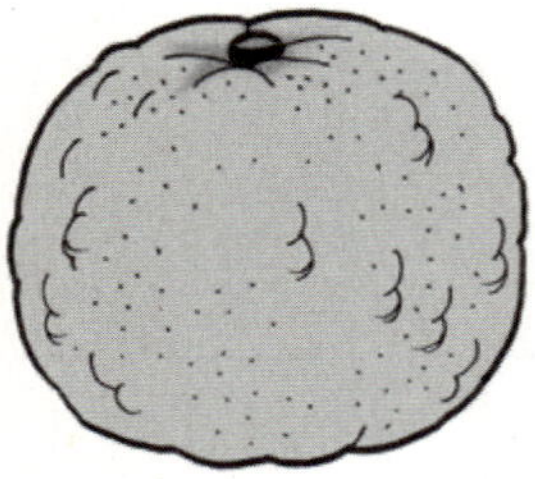

2. ____________________ 4. ____________________ 6. ____________________

2 Fill in the number for the population of each continent in Chinese.

北美洲 *Běi* Měizhōu:
30,000,000
1. ____________________

亚洲 Yàzhōu:
3,879,000,000
4. ________________

欧洲 Ōuzhōu:
723,000,000
2.________________

南美洲 Nán Měizhōu:
302,000,000
3.____________________

非洲 Fēizhōu:
62,000,000
5. ___________________

名字：________________________ 日期：____________

3 Match each sentence to its correct response.

A. 珍珍喜欢什么颜色？Zhēnzhēn xǐ.huān shén.me yán.sè?

B. 你的学校有多少学生？Nǐ.de xuéxiào yǒu duōshǎo xué.shēng?

C. 这条裙子打几折？Zhèi-tiáo qún.zi *dǎ* jǐ-zhé?

D. 这件咖啡色的大衣怎么样？Zhèi-jiàn kāfēi.sè .de dàyī zěn.meyàng?

E. 他要买什么颜色的衬衫？Tā yào mǎi shén.me yán.sè .de chènshān?

F. 你有几件牛仔裤？*Nǐ yǒu* jǐ-jiàn niúzǎikù?

G. 这件裤子没有折扣吗？Zhèi-jiàn kù.zi méi.yǒu zhékòu .ma?

H. 这件灰色的外套多少钱？Zhèi-jiàn huī.sè .de wàitào duōshǎo qián?

1. ________ 红色。Hóng.sè.
2. ________ 三件。Sān-jiàn.
3. ________ 灰色的。Huī.sè .de.
4. ________ 八点五折。Bā *diǎn* wǔ-zhé.
5. ________ 一千八百个。Yì-qiān bā-bǎi .ge.
6. ________ 不好意思，没有。Bù hǎoyì.sì, méi.yǒu.
7. ________ 两千八百块钱。Liǎng-qiān bā-bǎi-kuài qián.
8. ________ 我觉得很好看。Wǒ jué.de *hěn* hǎokàn

名字：________________________ 日期：____________

4 Match each person with the item of clothing he/she wants to purchanse.

1. _____ 

我想买一件有折扣的毛衣。
Wǒ xiǎng mǎi yí-jiàn yǒu zhékòu .de máoyī.

A. 

2. _____ 

我想买一件漂亮的裙子。
Wǒ xiǎng mǎi yí-jiàn piào.liàng .de qún.zi.

B. 

3. _____ 

我想买一件便宜一点儿的白色衬衫。
Wǒ xiǎng mǎi yí-jiàn pián.yí yì.diǎnr .de bái.sè chènshān.

C. 

4. _____ 

我想买一件连衣裙，价钱贵一点儿没关系。
Wǒ xiǎng mǎi yí-jiàn liányīqún, jiàqián guì yì.diǎnr méi guān.xì.

D. 

5 Choose the best answer.

1. _____ Which is the correct composition of Wu Xing (Five elements)?

   A. metal, wood, water, fire, earth
   B. gold, silver, water, fire, earth
   C. metal, wind, water, wood, fire

2. _____ Which is not a shared characteristic between Japanese kimonos and Chinese-style clothing?

   A. long skirts B. wide sleeves C. overlapping lapels

3. _____ Which of the following is not a correct representation of colors for the Chinese?

   A. White represents purity
   B. Purple represents royalty
   C. Yellow represents wealth

6 Read the following statements and answer the questions. (Note: you may need a calculator to do this exercise.)

1. 一台五千块钱的电脑，打八折，多少钱？
   Yì-tái wǔ-qiān kuài qián .de diànnǎo, dǎ bā-zhé, duō.shǎo qián?

   ____

2. 一辆十万块的车，打九折，多少钱？
   Yí-liàng shí-wàn kuài.de chē, *dǎ* jiǔ-zhé, duō.shǎo qián?

   ____

3. 一栋两百万的房子(*house*)，打五折，多少钱？
Yí-dòng *liǎng*-bǎi wàn .de fáng.zi, *dǎ* wǔ-zhé, duō.shǎo qián?

____

4. 一条三百块钱的长裤，打七折，多少钱？
Yì-tiáo sān-bǎi kuài qián .de chángkù, dǎ qī-zhé, duō.shǎo qián?

____

5. 一套八百块的西装，打三折，多少钱？
Yí-tào bā-bǎi kuài .de xīzhuāng, dǎ sān-zhé, duō.shǎo qián?

____

7 Fill in the original price and the discount.

Lì.zi: ￥ 500 → 10% off = ￥450

打 dǎ 九 折 zhé。

1. ￥ __________ → 15% off = ￥8,500

打 dǎ __________ 折 zhé。

2. ￥ __________ → 30% off = ￥4,200,000

打 dǎ __________ 折 zhé。

3. ￥ __________ → 25% off = ￥12,500,000

打 dǎ __________ 折 zhé。

4. ￥ __________ → 90% off = ￥1,000

打 dǎ __________ 折 zhé。

5. ￥ __________ → 60% off = ￥190,000

打 dǎ __________ 折 zhé。

8 Answer the following questions.

1. 你喜欢自己选衣服吗？*Nǐ* xǐ.huān zì*jǐ* xuǎn yī.fú .ma?

____

2. 你觉得什么颜色的裤子好看？Nǐ jué.de shén.me yán.sè .de kù.zi hǎokàn?

____

3. 一件九十块美金的漂亮衬衫，打五折，你买不买？
Yí-jiàn jiǔ.shí-kuài Měijīn .de piào.liàng chènshān, *dǎ* wǔ-zhé, *nǐ* mǎi bù mǎi?

____

名字：________________ 日期：__________

Unit 6 Lesson C

1 The people below describe the way they are dressed. Fill in the blanks with the corresponding adjectives.

旧 jiù	松 sōng	时髦 shímáo	紧 jǐn	老 lǎo	合身 héshēn

这件牛仔裤的大小刚好！
Zhèi-jiàn niúzǎikù .de dàxiǎo gāng hǎo!

1. ________________

这件衬衫是 M 号，可是我穿 XL 号的。Zhèi-jiàn chènshān shì M hào, kě.shì wǒ chuān XL hào .de.

3. ________________

这件外套我已经穿十年了！Zhèi-jiàn wàitào wǒ yǐ.jīng chuān shí-nián .le!

5. ________________

我昨天穿新的连衣裙，可是朋友说那件连衣裙是五十岁的人穿的！
Wǒ zuó.tiān chuān xīn .de liányīqún, kě.shì péng.yǒu shuō nèi-jiàn liányīqún shì wǔ.shí-suì .de rén chuān .de!

2. ________________

这件是这个月在百货商店买的新衣服，非常好看。
Zhèi-jiàn shì zhèi-.ge yuè zài bǎihuò shāngdiàn mǎi .de xīn yī.fú, fēicháng hǎokàn.

4. ________________

这件衬衫太大了，有没有小一点儿的？
Zhèi-jiàn chènshān tài dà .le, yǒu méi. *yǒu* xiǎo yìdiǎnr .de?

6. ________________

名字：________________ 日期：________

2 Match each question to its correct response.

A. 这件毛衣时髦吗？Zhèi-jiàn máoyī shímáo .ma?

B. 这件衬衫大小怎么样？Zhèi-jiàn chènshān dàxiǎo zěn.meyàng?

C. 你觉得这条牛仔裤好看吗？Nǐ jué.de zhèi-tiáo niúzǎikù hǎokàn .ma?

D. 这件外套有没有 38 号的？Zhèi-jiàn wàitào yǒu méi.yǒu sān.shíbā-hào .de?

E. 你想请谁来你的生日派对？*Nǐ xiǎng* qǐng shéi lái nǐ.de shēng.rì pàiduì?

F. 下次我们一起去玩，好吗？Xiàcì wǒ.mén yìqǐ qù wán, hǎo .ma?

G. 我穿什么颜色的衣服比较合适？Wǒ chuān shén.me yánsè .de yī.fú bǐjiào héshì?

1. ______ 红色。Hóng.sè.
2. ______ 我觉得不但好看，而且合身。Wǒ jué.de búdàn hǎokàn, érqiě héshēn.
3. ______ 好啊！没问题。Hǎo .a! Méi wèntí.
4. ______ 不好意思，没有。Bù hǎoyì.sī, méi.yǒu.
5. ______ 我想请小华、美文和国正。*Wǒ xiǎng qǐng* Xiǎohuá, Měiwén hé Guózhèng.
6. ______ 太紧了。Tài jǐn .le.
7. ______ 一点都不，我觉得。Yì.diǎn dōu bù, wǒ jué.de.

3 Use the pattern 不但……而且……*búdàn… érqiě…*to rewrite the sentences.

Lì.zi: 哥哥想打篮球，也想踢足球。
Gē.x *xiǎng* dǎ-lánqiú, *yě* xiǎng tī-zúqiú.
哥哥不但想打篮球，而且也想踢足球。
Gē.x búdàn *xiǎng* dǎ-lánqiú, ér*qiě yě* xiǎng tī-zúqiú.

1. 这家餐厅的菜又贵又难吃。Zhèi jiā cāntīng .de cài yòu guì yòu nánchī.

   ____

2. 姐姐上中文课，还上日文课。Jiě.x shàng Zhōngwén kè, hái shàng Rìwén kè.

   ____

3. 他的衬衫又松又旧。Tā.de chènshān yòu sōng yòu jiù.

   ____

4. 小英的牛仔裤又合身又好看。Xiǎoyīng .de niúzǎikù yòu héshēn yòu hǎokàn.

   ____

5. 他们不喜欢吃炸鸡，也不喜欢喝可乐。
   Tā.mén bù xǐ.huān chī zhájī, yě bù xǐ.huān hē kělè.

   ____

4 Look at the chart below and decide if each statement is true or false.

	瑛瑛 Yīngyīng	李明 Lǐmíng	世方 Shìfāng	小真 Xiǎozhēn	国华 Guóhuá
衬衫 chènshān		size 40		size 35	size38
外套 wàitào		size 42	size 42		size 40
连衣裙 liányīqún	size 37				
T 恤 tīxù	size 36	size 38		size 34	
牛仔裤 niúzǎikù	size 29			size 28	

1. ______ 瑛瑛穿三十七号的连衣裙。 Yīngyīng chuān sān.shíqī-hào .de liányīqún.

2. ______ 李明和国华都穿四十号的外套。

   Lǐmíng hé Guóhuá dōu chuān sì.shí-hào .de wàitào.

3. ______ 小真穿二十九号的牛仔裤太小。

   Xiǎozhēn chuān èr.shíjiǔ-hào .de niúzǎikù tài xiǎo.

4. ______ 世方穿四十二号的外套刚刚好。

   Shìfāng chuān sì.shí'èr-hào .de wàitào gāng.x hǎo.

5. ______ 瑛瑛穿二十九号的牛仔裤很合身。

   Yīngyīng chuān èr.shíjiǔ-hào .de niúzǎikù hěn héshēn.

6. ______ 国华穿四十号的衬衫有点儿松。

   Guóhuá chuān sì.shí-hào .de chènshān *yǒu*diǎnr sōng.

7. ______ 李明穿三十八号的 T 恤大小刚好。

   Lǐmíng chuān sān.shíbā-hào .de tīxù dàxiǎo gāng hǎo.

名字：________________________ 日期：____________

5 Choose the best answer.

1. ______ What is not one of the clothing sizes used in China?

   A. 号 *hào* B. 码 *mǎ* C. 型 *xíng*

2. ______ In what measurement are the labels of Chinese clothing sizes?

   A. inches B. centimeters C. meters

3. ______ Which of the following countries uses a different system of measurement for footwear?

   A. China B. France C. Japan

6 Answer the following questions.

1. 你觉得你很时髦吗？
   Nǐ jué.de *nǐ* hěn shímáo .ma?

   ____

2. 你喜欢合身的衣服还是松的衣服？
   Nǐ xǐ.huān héshēn .de yī.fú hái.shì sōng .de yī.fú?

   ____

3. 你喜欢自己去买衣服还是跟朋友一起去？
   Nǐ xǐ.huān zìjǐ qù mǎi yī.fú hái.shì gēn péng.yǒu yìqǐ qù?

   ____

4. 你喜欢成熟的衣服吗？
   Nǐ xǐ.huān chéng shú .de yī.fú .ma?

   ____

名字：________________________ 日期：____________

7 **The following is Lulu's April calendar and a description of her friends. She hasn't decided who she should invite to do each activity with her. Help her find the suitable person and write down the final decisions.**

星期一 Xīngqīyī	星期二 Xīngqī'èr	星期三 Xīngqīsān	星期四 Xīngqīsì	星期五 Xīngqīwǔ	星期六 Xīngqīliù	星期日 Xīngqīrì
1	2	3 去日本玩 qù Rìběn wán	4	5	6	7
8	9	10	11 法国音乐会 Fǎ.guó yīnyuèhuì	12	13	14
15 看电影 kàn-diànyǐng	16	17	18 游泳 yóuyǒng	19	20 茶店喝茶 chádiàn hē-chá	21
22	23	24 去中国餐馆 qù Zhōng.guó cānguǎn	25	26 买衣服 mǎi yī.fú	27	28

郑翔 Zhèng Xiáng：喜欢体育课，他的爱好是游泳。
Xǐ.huān tǐyù kè, tā.de àihào shì yóuyǒng.

林平 Lín Píng：很时髦，和 Lulu 一起修法文课。Hěn shímáo, hé Lulu yìqǐ xiū Fǎwén kè.

李华 Lǐ Huá：喜欢喝下午茶。星期六早上和 Lulu 一起上画画课。
Xǐ.huān hē xiàwǔchá. Xīngqīliù zǎo.shàng hé Lulu yìqǐ shàng huà.x kè.

张英 Zhāng Yīng：会说日文，喜欢日本文化(*culture*)。
Huì shuō Rìwén, xǐ.huān Rìběn wénhuà.

美芳 Měifāng：学中文两年，中文很好。不但喜欢中国文化，而且喜欢吃中国菜。
Xué Zhōngwén liǎng-nián, Zhōngwén hěn hǎo. Búdàn xǐ.huān Zhōng.guó wénhuà, érqiě xǐ.huān chī Zhōng.guó cài.

温红 Wēn Hóng：喜欢看电影，常常去图书馆看书。
Xǐ.huān kàn-diànyǐng, cháng.x qù túshūguǎn kàn-shū.

名字：________________ 日期：________

Follow the model, help Lulu jot down whom to invite and what to do on the following dates.

Lì.zi: 四月二十六日请林平跟我去买衣服。

Sìyuè èr.shíliù rì qǐng Lín Píng gēn wǒ qù mǎi yī.fú.

1. 四月一日 Sìyuè yī rì ～ 四月六日 Sìyuè liù rì

____

2. 四月十一日 Sìyuè shíyī rì

____

3. 四月十五日 Sìyuè shíwǔ rì

____

4. 四月十八日 Sìyuè shíbā rì

____

5. 四月二十日 Sìyuè èr.shí rì

____

6. 四月二十四日 Sìyuè èr.shísì rì

____

名字：________________ 日期：__________

Unit 6 Lesson D

1 Match each of the following pictures to the correct vocabulary word.

1. _____ 

A. 靴子
xuē.zi

2. _____ 

B. 袜子
wà.zi

3. _____ 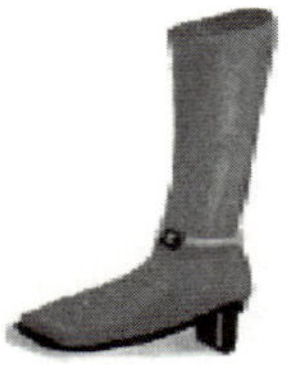

C. 夹脚脱鞋
jiā-jiǎo tuōxié

4. _____ 

D. 运动鞋
yùndòngxié

5. _____ 

E. 皮鞋
píxié

6. _____ 

F. 拖鞋
tuōxié

2 Fill in the blanks with the correct word from the box.

有型 yǒuxíng	套 tào	怎么样 zěn.meyàng		找 zhǎo
适合 shìhé	一点儿 yì.diǎnr	样 yàng	帮忙 bāngmáng	试试 shì.x

1. **A:** 请问你需要 Qǐngwèn nǐ xūyào____________吗.ma？

   B: 我想 *Wǒ* xiǎng____________这双咖啡色的靴子 zhèi-shuāng kāfēi.sè .de xuē.zi。

2. **A:** 这双运动鞋有没有大 Zhèi-shuāng yùndòngxié yǒu méiyǒu dà____________的.de？

   B: 有，请等一下。Yǒu, *qǐng* děng yí.xià.

3. **A:** 这 Zhèi____________西装 xīzhuāng____________？

   B: 很帅 Hěn shuài，很 hěn____________你 nǐ。

4. **A:** 你想 *Nǐ* xiǎng____________什么样的衣服 shén.meyàng .de yī.fú？

   B: 我想买白色的衬衫。Wǒ xiǎng mǎi bái.sè .de chènshān.

5. **A:** 你想找什么 *Nǐ* xiǎng zhǎo____________的裙子.de qún.zi？

   B: 我想买一件 Wǒ xiǎng mǎi yí-jiàn____________一点儿的裙子 yì.diǎnr .de qún.zi。

3 Look at the chart below and read each person's point of view towards the appearance of the famous people and figures below. Decide if each of the following statements is true or false. Check the internet if you want to know what each person or figure looks like.

	张庭 Zhāng Tíng	温虹 Wēn Hóng	国华 Guóhuá	世容 Shìróng
Audrey Hepburn	美丽 měilì	漂亮 piào.liàng	美丽 měilì	美丽 měilì
Lady Gaga	有型 yǒuxíng	时髦 shímáo	年轻 niánqīng	有型 yǒuxíng
Homer Simpson	丑 chǒu	老 lǎo	有意思 yǒu yì.sī	好玩儿 hǎowánr
Brad Pitt	帅 shuài	成熟 chéngshú	过时 guòshí	帅 shuài

1. ______ 大家都觉得 Audrey Hepburn 很好看。

   Dàjiā dōu jué.de Audrey Hepburn *hěn* hǎokàn.

2. ______ 温虹觉得 Lady Gaga 一点儿都不时髦。

   Wēn Hóng jué.de Lady Gaga yì.diǎnr dōu bù shímáo.

3. ______ 张庭觉得 Lady Gaga 不但时髦，而且还很有型。

   Zhāng Tíng jué.de Lady Gaga búdàn shímáo, érqiě hái *hěn* yǒuxíng.

4. ______ 世容觉得 Homer 很好玩儿。Shìróng jué.de Homer *hěn* hǎowánr.

5. ______ 国华觉得 Homer 又老又丑。Guóhuá jué.de Homer yòu lǎo yòu chǒu.

6. ______ 张庭和世容都觉得 Brad Pitt 很帅。

   Zhāng Tíng hé Shìróng dōu jué.de Brad Pitt hěn shuài.

7. ______ 没有人觉得 Brad Pitt 过时。Méi.yǒu rén jué.de Brad Pitt guòshí.

名字：____________________ 日期：__________

4 Rewrite each sentence using 一点儿 *yì.diǎnr* to modify the adjective.

Li.zi: 你们有没有辣的菜？Nǐ.mén yǒu méi.yǒu là .de cài?
你们有没有辣一点儿的菜？Nǐ.mén yǒu méi.yǒu là yì.diǎnr .de cài?

1. 昨天二十五度，今天二十六度。Zuó.tiān èr.shíwǔ-dù, jīn.tiān èr.shíliù-dù.

____

2. 这件睡衣是 S 号的，我穿 M 号的。Zhèi-jiàn shuìyī shì S-hào .de, wǒ chuān M-hào .de.

____

3. 姐姐想找帅的男朋友（*boyfriend*）。Jiě.x *xiǎng* zhǎo shuài .de nán péng.yǒu.

____

4. 他很累，所以不想吃太多东西。Tā hěn lèi, *suǒ*.yǐ bù xiǎng chī tài duō dōng.xī.

____

5. 这杯红茶不甜，我要喝甜的红茶。Zhèi-bēi hóngchá bù tián, wǒ yào hē tián .de hóngchá.

____

6. 我觉得拖鞋二十块太贵了，你们有十五块的吗？
Wǒ jué.de tuōxié èr.shí-kuài tài guì .le, nǐ.mén yǒu shíwǔ-kuài .de .ma?

____

名字：________________ 日期：________

5 Write a sentence using 最 *zuì* to describe each picture.

1. ______________________________

____

3. ______________________________

____

2. ______________________________

____

4. ______________________________

____

名字：________________________ 日期：__________

6 Describe how each of the following people are dressed. Follow the model.

Lì.zi: **A:** 他穿什么衣服？Tā chuān shén.me yī.fú?
B: 他穿一件很松的 T 恤和很大的牛仔裤。
Tā chuān yí-jiàn hěn sōng .de tīxù hé hěn dà .de niúzǎikù.

1. **A:** 她是一个什么样的学生？
Tā shì yí-.ge shén.meyàng .de xuéshēng?

B: ______________________________

2. **A:** 这是一双什么样的靴子？
Zhè .shì yì-shuāng shén.meyàng .de xuē.zi?

B: ______________________________

3. **A:** 这是一个什么样的男人？
Zhè .shì yí-.ge shén.meyàng .de nánrén?

B: ______________________________

7 Choose the best answer.

1. ____ Which of the following is not a correct description about Wangfujing?

   A. It has long history.
   B. It is a pedestrian area.
   C. It is a famous residential street.

2. ____ Which is not the silk capital in China?

   A. Suzhou B. Guizhou C. Hangzhou

3. ____ Which of the following descriptions is not correct about the Chinese silk culture?

   A. Silk production originated more than 3,000 years ago.
   B. Silk production was near the lower end of Yangtze River.
   C. Silk has been a favorite of China's aristocracy and merchants.

8 Answer the following questions in Pinyin according to your own situation.

1. 夏天的时候，你穿夹脚脱鞋吗？Xià.tiān .de shíhòu, nǐ chuān jiā-jiǎo tuōxié .ma?

____

2. 你有几双鞋子？*Nǐ yǒu* jǐ-shuāng xié.zi?

____

3. 冬天的时候，你穿不穿靴子？Dōng.tiān .de shíhòu, nǐ chuān bù chuān xuē.zi?

____

